Praise for *The Grandmother Paradox*

"Packed with action, drama, comedy and final revelations, Nikel's new chapter is an extraordinary continuation of her time travel universe."

—Stephanie Wexler, Tangent Online

"Fans will appreciate Nikel's signature attention to detail and atmosphere."

—Publishers Weekly

Praise for *The Continuum*

"Nikel's inventive spin on time travel and eye for sumptuous detail make her writing a treat to read."

—Publishers Weekly

"*The Continuum* packs a staggering amount of well drawn world-building into a short space, making for enough time travel adventure to launch a series...full of heart, humor, and thrilling action and adventure scenes that make for a fun, fast read."

—*Foreword Reviews*

"Nikel's time travel narrative is brisk and energetic, with a relatively straightforward and action oriented plot...those interested in a light and enjoyable SF read in the style of popular time-travel tropes such as *Doctor Who* should give it a look."

—*IndiePicks Magazine*

The Grandmother Paradox

A Place in Time Novella

(Book #2)

Wendy Nikel

World Weaver Press

THE GRANDMOTHER PARADOX

Wendy Nikel
Copyright © 2018 Wendy Nikel.

This is a work of fiction; characters and events are either fictitious or used fictitiously.

Published by World Weaver Press, LLC
Albuquerque, NM
www.WorldWeaverPress.com
Editor: Rhonda Parrish

Cover layout and design by Sarena Ulibarri.
Cover images used under license from Shutterstock.com.

*

First edition: July 2018
ISBN-13: 978-0998702285

Also available as an ebook

THE GRANDMOTHER PARADOX

THE PLACE IN TIME TRAVEL AGENCY'S
TEN ESSENTIAL RULES OF TIME TRAVEL

1. Travelers must return to their original era as scheduled.

2. Travelers are prohibited from Jumping to any time they have already experienced.

3. Travel dates must be prior to the traveler's birth.

4. Travel within the Black Dates is prohibited.*

5. Only pre-approved objects may be taken into the past.

6. Travelers are prohibited from disclosing information about PITTA or its excursions.

7. Travelers are prohibited from disclosing any foreknowledge to people of the past.

8. Travelers must avoid all unnecessary fraternization with people of past eras.

9. Extractions must occur in secure, unobservable locations.

10. After Extraction, clients must immediately return their Wormhole Devices to PITTA headquarters.

*for complete list of Black Dates, see PITTA handbook Appendix B.

CHAPTER ONE: APRIL 15, 2113

I haven't seen the old man in a hundred years, but when the doorbell chimes and the screen lights up, there he is. He can't be much older than the last time we met—a few years, at the most—but seeing him *here*, instead of in that darkened bunker that blinked and hummed with that crazy machine of his, was a bit akin to seeing a circus elephant wandering around the airtrain station. When I open the door, he's studying my 22nd century apartment building with its seamless façade and rotating solar panels that look nothing like the ones of his day.

"Agent Chandler!" he greets me.

"Been a long time since someone called me that."

He offers a handshake and I take it unthinkingly, quickly falling into old habits in this strange out-of-time moment.

"Of course," he says. "So good to see you again. Do you mind if I step inside? We have some important matters to discuss, and your front stoop perhaps isn't the best place to do so."

"Sure." What choice do I have? He's sure to draw curious looks with those horn-rimmed spectacles, flat cap, tweed jacket, and corduroy pants. You'd think Dr. Wells, of all people, would be more careful about what he wears while time-traveling. Then again, his business is in the vast reaches of the past, not the shiny, synthetic future where I currently live. *No, I think, not the future.* How long before I stop thinking of it like that?

"Make yourself at home." I gesture vaguely toward my living room, seeing it now as Dr. Wells would: the memory foam futon made of 100% recycled, hypoallergenic materials, the empty biodegradable food containers from the past week's worth of Punch-In meals, a scattering of personal visual devices (which to him probably look like regular silver sunglasses) lying in various states of disrepair. I swipe up some of Dodge's half-completed study cubes off the coffee table to clear a space for my guest. "Can I get you something to drink?"

Dr. Wells shakes his head, settling himself onto the futon and looking so out of place I can't help but grin. I'd probably laugh out loud were it not for the feeling like quicksand settling in my stomach. The last time I'd seen him, he'd slipped me a warning that my employer was plotting to kill me. The fact that he's *here*, paying a visit to me *now*, means something is very wrong.

I settle into an armchair I've always thought was uncomfortable but can't get rid of; my adopted son Dodge loves it and I wouldn't dream of denying him something as simple as a favorite chair after all he's been through. "What's up, Doc?"

Dr. Wells looks up, startled, and gives me a sad-looking grin. "Did she tell you she used to say that? It was our little joke."

"Who, Elise?" When I'd known her, she'd been so serious, so focused on returning me to the 21st century that I find it hard to picture her laughing and joking around with her boss like that. "Afraid that's a side of her I didn't get to see. How is she?"

"She's safe. It's probably better you don't know more than that. You know how it is in this business."

I nod. That's all I need to know. It's been a year now since she helped Dodge and me escape from an experimental colony in space before it was destroyed by an asteroid. My former employers had hired her—a professional time traveler who worked at Dr. Wells's clandestine time travel agency—to track me down and kick me back to the 21st century where I belonged. I'll be forever grateful to her for letting me slip away and telling my employers that I'd been lost with the colony.

"Actually," Dr. Wells says, fiddling with the watch on his wrist, "the issue I've come to discuss with you today involves her."

My heart skips a beat. "You said she's okay, though, right?"

"Oh, yes," Dr. Wells nods, his head bobbing comically. "That is… She's not in any immediate harm's way. Not directly. Though indirectly…"

"Tell me." My fingers tighten around the arms of the chair, and I force them off and wipe my sweaty palms on my silvery suit. If anything were to happen to Elise… Not that she can't take care of herself, but still… "What happened?"

"Oh, nothing yet," the wide-eyed scientist says, taking off his glasses and polishing them on the hem of his shirt. "Though with time travel, you understand how muddled these things become."

"Fine, then what *will* happen? Just tell me what the problem is, and I'll do whatever I can to help."

Dr. Wells nods grimly. "I knew I could count on you."

What have I just agreed to?

Never mind that. After all Elise has done to help me, I'd do anything to help her. Although… My eyes wander to some bricks Dodge left on the table. There's plenty of PVD games that mimic interlocking tactile construction, and the vintage toys cost me an arm and a leg at an antique shop, but every eight-year-old boy needs his own LEGOs.

"How long will this take?" I ask.

"Goodness, I have no idea. Days… weeks… months, perhaps."

"Months?" My eyebrows shoot up in surprise.

"Oh, yes. Elise told me about your ward. Don't you worry. I'll have you back here before he gets home from school."

"How do you intend to do that?"

"Time travel," Dr. Wells says with a wink. He digs in his jacket pocket. "I've improved the methods a bit since your last travels; the annual interval is still the most energy-efficient way to travel, but if you don't mind a few side effects—nausea, vertigo, and the like—I can get you back within twenty-four hours of when you left. Now, we'll just pop on back to my office and I'll fill you in on the details while you select your wardrobe. Not knowing how long you'll be gone, we'd best ensure a good fit."

"Your office?" I ask. "In New York, you mean?"

In the past. My true present.

Dr. Wells pulls out a set of palm-sized spheres so glossy and black they remind me of the endless, empty sky. The last time I saw one of those was with Elise, back on the space colony, minutes before it burst into a billion tiny shards of light. I draw in my breath.

Dr. Wells places the orb in my hand and closes my fingers around it. It feels cold and hard and impossibly smooth. A tremor of apprehension works its way down my spine.

"Sure about this, old man?" I smile, one of my common defense mechanisms. "It has to be me?"

"I'm afraid so. There are very few people who know that Elise escaped the *Continuum* disaster, and—for her sake—it's best if we keep it that way. Just press the button when you're ready."

Dodge's boots sit beside the door, their soles cracked and fasteners fraying. He needs a new pair soon; the kid is going through another growth spurt.

"And you swear I'll come right back here, when it's all said and done?" My voice catches, and I clear my throat, trying to recapture my usual steady demeanor. "Right back to this time, this place?"

Dr. Wells meets my eye. "I swear."

I know about his Rules, the foremost being that all travelers must return to their own era of origin. We both know I'm not really from the 22nd century, that I was born in 1985 and ought to be living back in the age of iPhones and Segways, rather than this shining era of clean energy, holographic interfaces, and instant food delivery a hundred years in the future.

"I know it goes against your first Rule."

"It does, but I think you'll find that what I'm going to ask you to do breaks a number of my Rules. There are times when we must do what we have to, following the spirit of the law, if not the letter." He gives me a look I find oddly unreadable. "Remember that."

"Can I leave him a note? Just in case—" I break off at the sight of Dr. Wells's frown. "I'll tell him something came up for work. I do computer programming—freelance, so sometimes I have to travel to visit clients. This may be dangerous, right?"

Dr. Wells hesitates. "It may be."

"Then I need him to know, if something happens, that I meant to come back. That I didn't desert him."

Reluctantly, the old man nods. "No details, though."

"No details," I agree, passing him the device and scrambling to find one of Dodge's note tablets before Dr. Wells changes his mind. With a shaking hand, I try to find the words and eventually settle on some: "Hey, Dodge. Something big came up. Not sure how long I'll be. If you need anything, go to the Richardsons' down the hall; they've been such good neighbors, I'm sure they won't mind helping you out."

I hesitate before signing my name to it. Recently, Dodge has taken to calling me "dad," a name I'm not sure I deserve.

"Ready?" Dr. Wells asks.

I sign the note with a "love, Dad" and set it aside, my heart racing, before I can second-guess myself. If all goes well, I'll be back here before he sees it anyway.

Dr. Wells offers me the device again, and my thumb finds its way to the button that'll send me whipping back through time to the 21st century. I don't want to go. Yet I trust him; after all, he was the one who'd warned me about my old employers' true intentions. And for

the sake of the woman who saved my life...
    I press the button and the world bursts into light.

CHAPTER TWO: APRIL 15, 2016

The spinning slows. Suddenly, everything stops.

The office we've landed in is every bit Dr. Wells's, from the antique desk taking up the center of the room—covered with every kind of paper and writing utensil imaginable—to the one-of-a-kind artwork on the walls. I land in front of one depicting some long-ago battle and know that all I'd have to do is ask and Dr. Wells would give me a full graduate-level lecture on the event, as well as each of the historical figures depicted.

"You quite all right down there?" Dr. Wells's face appears over the pile of papers, a hint of concern tugging at his oversized brows and a bead of sweat lingering on his mustache.

"Just a little disoriented." I pull myself up to a nearby chair and take a deep breath. My head throbs and my body feels off-balanced, as if somehow the world beneath me is spinning just slightly off-kilter from how it does a hundred years later. "Home, sweet 21st century."

I'd never been to the Place in Time Travel Agency before, but I knew it was in New York City—a fact made all too clear as the hum and buzz of the city leaks through the office's single window. Cars rumble by, horns honk, and somewhere nearby, a large vehicle backs up with an incessant *beep, beep, beep, beep.* I'd forgotten how noisy this era was, with its combustion engines and constant construction, the incessant chatter of cell phones and machines. It makes me want to press my hands to my ears.

"Tea?" Dr. Wells asks, offering me a steaming mug that he seems to have pulled out of nowhere. Either that, or he prepared it before jumping to the future, knowing I'd need something to calm my nerves upon my return. Either way, I appreciate the gesture.

"I'm usually a coffee-drinker, you know," I say as I sip from the mug. It's some flavor I haven't tasted or smelled in a long time; I can't even remember what it's called anymore. Were the herbs it's made from lost in the last century? Or did they just go out of style? "Good stuff, though, this."

Dr. Wells nods absently as he flits around the office, gathering up a collection of items in front of me. A suit, pressed and black. A bowler hat. A billfold, stuffed with paper dollars. A pocket watch.

"Looks like I'm either going back further," I say, "or vintage clothing has circled back into style since I've been gone."

Dr. Wells looks up as if he'd forgotten I'm here. "Oh! Yes, that's right. You need a debriefing. Where to begin?" He sighs and collapses back into his chair. "How much do you know about what we do here?"

"Just what Elise told me. Your clients pay the big bucks for you to send them into the past on little vacations or getaways or research trips or whatever. All very hush-hush, referrals only."

"Yes, yes." Dr. Wells nods. "I suppose that does sum it up nicely. Now, as you might imagine, being in this sort of business does have its own particular... hazards."

"Clients getting in over their heads, you mean?"

"Well, that too. Though that's what we have our Retrievers, like Elise, for." He sighs. "It's been difficult to find a replacement for her. She really was one of the most skilled time travelers I've worked with. There's one girl I believe is showing promise, but— Never mind that. No, I was referring to the dangers here in the present. People who have discovered what we do and wish to exploit my technology for their own purposes."

"Right." I shift in my chair. That's precisely what the Trial Undertaking Bureau, or TUB, had done back when I still worked for them. I was lucky I'd gotten out when I did, before things got too messy. Yet something about Dr. Wells's expression makes me wonder. "TUB isn't causing trouble for you again, are they?"

"I'm afraid so. Or at least, I assume it's them. See, their interest in the future revolved solely around the *Continuum*."

I nod. That was the name of the space colony TUB sent me to assess. They'd wanted to evaluate the outcome of their investment— their legacy.

"So they found out about the disaster? That couldn't have been welcome news."

"Yes, and unfortunately, they've come to entirely the wrong conclusion. Shortly after Elise's return, TUB sent another of my Retrievers into the future and the information he brought back led them to believe that, instead of Retrieving you, Elise sabotaged the colony to ensure its destruction."

"That's ridiculous. Why would anyone think she'd do something like that?"

"Tell me—what's being reported in your time, a year after the disaster?"

"Not much," I admit. "It's still under investigation."

"When the *Continuum*'s Governing Board finally releases its report, it will include testimony from a security guard who claims he pursued an unidentified, unauthorized woman through the colony's restricted areas just before the order to evacuate. The Governing Board—desperate to defend themselves against charges of neglect and mismanagement—will latch onto this idea and within days of this announcement, this unknown woman will be the most-wanted terrorist of the 22nd century. I contacted you before this all went public so that you wouldn't be alarmed."

I curse beneath my breath. "Is she in danger?"

"I've sent her into the past," Dr. Wells says, "where she's living under another name as a contemporary. No one, not even TUB, should be able to trace her. However…"

Here, he holds out a folder. Inside are copies of census records, birth records, marriage certificates, and a few faded black-and-white photos.

"What's all this?" I ask, turning over an image of a young girl with a pug on her lap.

"That," Dr. Wells says. "Is Elise's great-great-grandmother. She was born in 1875. She is the most vulnerable of her direct ancestors."

My head jerks upward. "What do you mean, most vulnerable? What is TUB planning?"

"I don't know," Dr. Wells admits. "They've gone dark. I haven't been contacted since my Retriever brought back that report. However, I have friends in genealogical libraries and research centers around the world, as well as those who work with all the major search engines. It's important, you see, that Retrievers not cross paths with their direct ancestors. That sort of entanglement can cause all sorts of trouble. Perhaps you've heard of a Grandfather Paradox?"

It sounds vaguely familiar, but Dr. Wells doesn't give me time to respond before continuing.

"It deals with the matter of what would happen if a time traveler were to kill his own grandfather before his father was conceived. There could be no time traveler then, could there? Would the traveler cease to exist and therefore be unable to kill his grandfather? Or would time splinter into an alternate path, leaving the traveler no present to return to in which he exists? Some hypothesize that a paradox like that would unravel the universe. You see what trouble that might cause?"

I nod mutely, still staring down at the image.

"I am concerned that TUB may want to test that theory. If they cannot get their hands on Elise herself, they may simply attempt to eliminate one of her direct ancestors instead." He grabs one of the pages from my hands, upon which is a family tree. Slowly, he tears the sheet in half, severing the names on the top from those on the bottom. "Thus, destroying her family line and preventing her existence."

"And this is the ancestor they plan to go after?" I hold up the photograph. "How do you know?"

"I told you, I have well-connected friends. When TUB broke off communication with me, I asked them to keep an eye on Elise's family tree. Fortunately, one of them alerted me when she noticed a suspicious number of searches coming up for a particular young woman in the late 18th century. She was an only child, orphaned at a young age, and spent one summer in her early adult years on the road as a magician's assistant. I'm sure you can see the potential there. A young woman with no family, no roots, always a stranger in town, with no one to look out for her… It would be a golden opportunity for them, a time when she would be incredibly vulnerable."

"Yes, I see, " I say, frowning. "But what do you need me for? What could I do?"

"Haven't you been listening?" Dr. Wells says, pushing his glasses up farther on his nose. "I suspect they mean to kill her, and I need you to go back there and stop them."

CHAPTER THREE: APRIL 15, 1893

My body jerks to a stop.

The DeLorean Box—Dr. Wells's time travel machine—has disappeared, replaced by brilliant sunlight and the chattering of birds. My head feels like it's been run over by an airtrain, and I reach into my pocket to ensure that the Wormhole Device—the dark orb that's my ticket home—is nestled safely in my pressed suit.

I lie there for a moment, wondering what I've gotten myself into. Who does Dr. Wells think I am? The Terminator (the one from the second movie, obviously)? If so, hopefully protecting Elise's great-great-grandmother won't prove quite as dangerous as protecting John Connor. And hopefully she isn't as irritating as the kid in that movie. At any rate, I'm a computer geek, not a bodyguard. What am I doing in a place like this, decades before the first computer will be invented? I must be out of my mind.

Groaning, I push myself upright. First things first: figure out where I am.

According to Dr. Wells, this tiny Midwestern town on the shores of Lake Huron is the next stop on the circuit of the Amazing Velés, the traveling magician whom Elise's ancestor, Juliette Argent, has been hired to assist.

So far, all I can see, though, is cornfield after endless cornfield, with little green plants bursting out of the ground all around me. I brush off my dirtied trousers, check the sky, and start off in what might be a northerly direction, already thrown off that I can't just check that fact with a few taps of my PVDs.

It's been a long time since I've found myself in such a rustic place. Dodge and I, in our shimmery city of the future, hardly have any reason to leave our self-sufficient little neighborhood, much less the city limits. Maybe I ought to take the kid to see the countryside sometime. Though in my time, it won't look or sound or smell like this vast sea of grain—so much is run by automated systems in the future that even in sparsely populated areas, there'd be the hum of irrigation pipes beneath our feet and quality control drones taking measurements overhead. Here, everything is achingly still.

By the time I reach the bare, dusty road that runs like a stripped electrical wire into town, I'm sweaty and tired. The 19th century clothing Dr. Wells loaned me doesn't wick moisture like the synthetic stuff I'm used to back home, and I cringe at the dark stains already forming in the armpits of my jacket. Yuck. Great first impression I'll make, waltzing up to the little town's spring carnival. I shrug out of the outer layer and throw it over my shoulder.

A wagon rattles up from behind, emerging from among the sprouting grain and churning up a brown cloud of dust. I hop into the ditch and watch as it passes. The small, smudge-faced children wave, their legs dangling off the back, and I smile in return. It's hard to imagine someone plotting a murder in a place that looks so much like a Norman Rockwell painting. Still, I'll have to keep my guard up for TUB's men.

The fairgrounds are easy to find. Horses, sheep, and chickens wander noisily about between rows of hand-constructed booths advertising games and tests of strength and skill. Kids rush by in sunhats and shirts that were maybe once some shade of white, clutching the hands of younger siblings behind them.

The aroma of fresh food fills the air: sweet and savory, meat on a stick, pretzels, and all kinds of candies and baked goods. My stomach grumbles. How long has it been since breakfast, when I ordered two omelets through the Punch-In system for Dodge and myself?

I ought to buy something to eat. Corn on the cob, dripping with butter? Fresh apple pies with brown sugar sprinkled on top? Fried chicken? The fair's offerings all sound amazing, but when I reach into my jacket pocket, my gut sinks. The Wormhole Device is still there, but the billfold is gone.

Frantic, I check the other pockets. I even scan the ground around me, though there's no way it's there. If I dropped it, it'd have been when I landed in this era or when I'd thrown the jacket off, way back in that cornfield, now miles away. It'd all been so open, so empty, and I'd walked so far. There's no way I'd find it again. I run my fingers through my hair. Great. What now?

Dr. Wells had recommended that I get a job with the traveling magician so it won't seem suspicious that I'm following them across the Midwest but, even assuming all goes well, I'll need to eat before my first paycheck. I need to eat *tonight*. What will I do? What *can* I do? What would Elise do?

A gathering crowd catches my eye. Excited spectators press in on some sort of rowdy event around half a dozen looming poles and, despite my recent setback, curiosity gets the best of me.

"What's going on here?" I ask a man to my side as I crane my neck to peer over the crowd.

"Pole-climbing competition."

Huh. "Is there a prize?"

"Biggest prize of the day: a hundred dollars cash."

A hundred dollars. Admittedly, I have no idea what that means in 21st century dollars or 22nd century credits, but it ought to be enough to get by until I can secure a job with the Amazing Velés.

"Are they still accepting competitors?" I ask.

"You'd better hurry," the whiskered man says, pressing me

forward into the crowd.

I mutter my apologies and weave my way to the wooden fence separating the spectators from the participants.

"Anyone else want to test their skill?" the barker calls.

"I'll do it!"

"Good! Good!" The barker's an enormous man with a handlebar mustache and a suit two sizes too small. He directs me to the pole nearest the crowd, and—as I throw my jacket over a fence rail and scramble to roll up my sleeves—he plows through the rules. "All competitors must have one foot on the ground until the whistle is blown, at which point they will begin their climb. There's a bell at the top of each 40-foot pole, and the first person to ring the bell goes home with the prize. Ready?"

The crowd cheers. I nod.

"Good luck, son," the barker slaps my back and jerks his head at something over my shoulder. "You're going up against a crowd favorite."

I strain to see who the barker's referring to, but before I get a chance, he starts counting down.

"Focus," I mutter, surveying the spruce pole. Crowd favorite or not, I have to win if I want to eat tonight.

"Five... four..." shouts the crowd. "Three... two..."

At the sound of the whistle, I start climbing. The pole's essentially just a tree trunk with the branches chopped off, so the trick is to wrap my arms around it and shimmy upward, using the meager natural footholds it provides. I try to remember the rock-climbing lessons I took at the state-of-the-art gym back in the 22nd century, with a bio-sensors suit measuring my body's functions and an AI personal trainer in my ear, giving me tips and encouragement. It doesn't take long to realize that this is nothing like that.

From the corner of my eye, I see a competitor on a nearby pole slowly falling behind, and it gives me a confidence boost. I've got this. My muscles have been trained by the most high-tech AI, the most advanced machines. Cheers go up from the crowd, but when I chance a glance below, their attention isn't focused on me, but on the competitor behind me—the one the barker called the "crowd favorite."

I'm nearly to the top. Just a few more arms' lengths. Below, the crowd is whistling and hooting, hollering and yelling, and the frenzy drives me to climb faster, faster. I reach up, stretching to grasp the bell—

From somewhere behind, another bell rings just before mine.

Second place.

I wrap my legs around the pole and wipe my brow, fighting back disappointment. Second place. One second too late, and now not only will I have nothing to eat this evening, I'll have to sleep—out under the stars, most likely—in torn and sweaty clothing. What had seemed like the perfect solution at the time, in retrospect, feels pretty stupid.

I begin my careful descent from the pole, trying not to tear my pants any further. Meanwhile, on the ground, the crowd is still going wild with excitement for the winner. I pause to wipe some more sweat from my eyes, shifting my weight and leaning around to catch a glimpse of the man who'd beat me out.

"And our winner today," the barker announces from below, "our crowd favorite, who's already won the ax-throwing competition and the butter-churning competition—"

The crowd howls with laughter.

Butter-churning?

"—the fine little lady who's taken our fair by storm—"

Fine little lady? I jerk around and catch a glimpse of the barker raising the arm of a slim, dark-haired young woman, who beams out at the crowd.

"—Juliette Argent!"

Elise's great-great grandmother looks up and flashes a brilliant smile at me that seems equal parts apology and boast. I'm suddenly lightheaded, and my fingers slip from the tree bark. With a cry of surprise, I plummet to the ground.

CHAPTER FOUR

I don't black out entirely, though I might prefer that over witnessing the fuss the crowd makes. They press in with gaping mouths and arms reaching to steady me as I struggle to catch my breath. Once upright, it's like gravity goes wonky on me, and I nearly knock over the men trying to support me. They lower me to a seated position and barrage me with a sea of questions.

"Are you all right?"

"Bit dizzy there, eh?"

"How many fingers am I holding up?"

"Anyone know if this bloke has family here today?"

"What's yer name, son?"

I can't do much more than try to grin it off as I struggle to shake away the black specks hovering at the edges of my vision. I squeeze my eyes shut and when I open them again, the dark-haired woman is standing directly over me, her head tipped in scrutiny, like she can tell my clothing's just a costume. That I'm just playing a part. That I don't really belong here.

"Give him some room." She waves her hand about to break up the crowd and kneels beside me. "Are you all right?"

I try to speak, but my mouth is dry, my head's still spinning, and my heart's beating wildly in my chest. I can't tell if my disorientation's from the fall, the landing, or the intensity of the woman's eyes on me. She gestures to some men. "You two help me get him over to the wagons where he can lie down."

The men each grab one of my arms and lead me away, following the hypnotic swish of the magician's assistant's braid.

"Wait!" I say. "My jacket!"

Juliette glances around, then marches back over to the fence and grabs the jacket herself. I cringe as she flings it carelessly over her arm, but the Wormhole Device remains tucked safely inside as she leads the sorry bunch of us down the dusty path, weaving between carts of fresh vegetables and down a row of worn wagons on the edge of the fairgrounds.

"Right in there." Juliette gestures to a covered wagon of sorts, where a few wooden crates function as steps up to a cozy room, where thick canvas serves as a shield from the elements.

The men deposit me upon the bed, which is really just a pallet covered with blankets and a layer of hay as a mattress. I'm still feeling dizzy, so I lean back and rest my head against the pillow, breathing in the scent of hay and… what is that? Lavender?

"Technically, I'm not supposed to have men in here," Juliette says sharply, pouring a bit of water from a pitcher into a delicate teacup. "But Viggo's wagon is the only other place I know with a bed, and he keeps his dog Brutus tied up there while we're at shows to discourage thieves. Believe me, you wouldn't want to cross that beast. Nearly bit my hand off when I tried to pet it." She offers me the teacup, and I push myself upright to take it, her fingers brushing mine in the process.

"I'm Juliette, by the way."

"Chandler." I sip the water, somehow managing to slosh half of it down the front of my shirt. Juliette turns away, but not before I see her smile at my clumsiness. I suppose I should be grateful that she finds me amusing right now.

"You have any family out there I should hunt down to come care for you?" She jerks her head toward the open flap, where outside, the crowds bustle by.

"No. No, I came alone today. I take it you work at the fair?" I ask, trying to act casual. The last thing I want is for her to think I'm some creep who knows more about her than I ought to.

"I suppose I do." She wrings out a wet cloth into the basin and holds it out. "Here, put this on your head. I just joined up with Viggo—sorry, the Amazing Velés, I suppose I ought to call him—not too long ago. I'm his assistant."

"So this is your wagon?" I glance around the space with new curiosity. It's neat and tidy, with few furnishings or decorations, and no personal items besides a battered brass cage with a bird inside that tips his head at me and chirps.

"Viggo's, technically. It used to be his former assistant's, but she up and eloped back in Cleveland last season." She hoists herself onto the chest of drawers and rests on the edge of it. Then, as if realizing how unladylike she appears, sitting there swinging her legs in her brown trousers, she daintily crosses her ankles beneath her.

"Isn't he worried you'll do the same?"

Juliette rolls her eyes, but her cheeks color with such warmth and loveliness that it only proves my point. Elise was an attractive woman, no doubt, but she had a plainness about her, too, which allowed her to blend into crowds easily. Her great-great grandmother, though... with those big, expressive eyes and her lips, so quick to smile... She'd stand out anywhere.

"Our first show is this evening," she says, evading my question. "You ought to come. That is, if you're feeling well enough by then."

She turns those big eyes on me, and I feel as though I've gotten the wind knocked out of me again.

I struggle to sit up. I can't think straight in here. I need fresh air, somewhere that isn't heady with lavender and where those bright, intelligent eyes aren't on me, studying my every move. If I stay in here much longer, I don't know that I'll be able to keep from confessing everything to her. "I really should be going."

"You ought to stay. I'll admit, I feel rather responsible for you. If I hadn't distracted you while you were climbing down that pole—"

"I wouldn't want to get you in trouble with your new boss."

"Oh, never mind him," she says, waving a hand carelessly. "I'm always taking in strays: lost dogs, abandoned kittens. Peeps there is a sparrow I've been nursing back to health; he's just about strong enough to go free. Viggo and I grew up together, so he understands. And if not—" Here she shrugs carelessly. "Then I'll just make my way down to Chicago and find work there. There's bound to be other performers at the World's Fair there who need assistants. I'd really like to be an acrobat, mind you, but everyone's told me Barnum and Bailey won't even take a second look at anyone without some experience in showbiz. I figured I'd spend a year on the circuit with Viggo first, and he was gracious enough to give me the opportunity."

"Well if your acrobatic skills are anything like your climbing skills, I'm sure you'd do great."

She glances over her shoulder. "Do me a favor?"

"Sure."

"Don't mention that to Viggo."

"About the competition? Why not? You were fantastic."

"I wasn't supposed to win."

"What do you mean?"

"It's one of his rules. He said I could play the games at the fairs and carnivals we visit, but I'm not supposed to win. We're supposed to let the locals take home the prize, but I got a bit carried away. I wear a wig on stage during the magic show, so I don't think anyone else would recognize me. Oh. You don't think those men who helped you in here will make the connection, do you?" She bites her thumbnail thoughtfully.

"Nah," I assure her. "But what about the ax-throwing and butter-churning?"

"I might have gotten carried away on those, too."

Her expression is so sincerely remorseful, so innocent, that I laugh. My head throbs and I press the heel of my hand against it. "Ouch."

"Sorry! Sorry," Juliette says, sliding down from the chest of drawers. "I ought to let you rest, rather than chatting your ear off like this. I'll be back in a few hours to check up on you."

Before I can protest, Juliette slips gracefully from the wagon, flicking the canvas tent flap shut behind hcr and leaving me alone with nothing but the muffled noises of the fair around me and her lavender scent upon the pillow.

CHAPTER FIVE

I wake, my head still throbbing, to a redhead standing over me with a piping hot plate of food. It isn't until I look into her eyes that I recognize Juliette in a wig and a bathrobe.

"I'd stay and eat with you," she says as she flutters about the room like a startled moth, "but I have to finish getting ready or I'll be late for the first show."

My head swims as I try to sit up, and by the time I've accomplished that task, she's gone.

I eat quickly, not wanting to miss any of the act, and afterward, I weave my way across the dusty fairground, following the crowd of eager townsfolk to a small stage with a scarlet curtain drawn across it and a banner bearing the name, "The Amazing Velés."

As I wait for Juliette's entrance, my thumb finds the smooth surface of the Wormhole Device in my pocket. I wonder what Dodge is doing right now, then have the gut-churning realization that Dodge won't be born for two hundred years, that he isn't doing *anything* right now, at least not in the physical sense.

You'd think I'd be used to this time travel stuff by now: this strange, in-between experience where I can pinch myself and know I'm alive, but no one else I've ever known is yet.

The Amazing Velés takes the stage just as the sun dips itself into the bay, and as he performs his opening acts, I study the crowd. Men in bowler hats smoke pipes and exchange jokes. Women shush small children clinging to their skirts. Young men jostle one another playfully. Everyone is in a pleasant mood, and no one stands out as suspicious. Still, if Dr. Wells believes that TUB is coming for Juliette, I'd better keep my guard up.

Finally, the Amazing Velés—a tall, thin young man with a handlebar mustache, whom I'd only been half-watching—announces that he's going to make his assistant appear from behind a magical curtain. He raises it above his head, pulls it aside with a flourish, and there she stands.

In addition to the curly wig and a face full of makeup, which makes her expressive eyes and lips look even larger, Juliette is wearing a red dress adorned with feathers and a matching headdress. The crowd—particularly the men—hoot and whistle, but she's got the poise and confidence of a pro, and her smile doesn't waver.

Over the next half-hour, the Amazing Velés levitates her, saws her in half, and locks her in a trunk where, upon opening the lid, she disappears, only to appear moments later at my elbow. She winks and tweaks me playfully on the shoulder before parading back to the stage. It isn't the greatest magic show I've seen—in any century—and I've read enough on Harry Houdini to know how most the tricks work, but with Juliette's gaze flicking over to meet mine throughout the show, I can't look away.

"For tonight's final trick," the Amazing Velés announces, "my assistant will be performing a feat of daring and courage, of quickness and skill… one of the most dangerous stunts known to mankind. The bullet-catch!"

The Amazing Velés pulls out an ivory-handled pistol, and my stomach drops. He makes a show of loading the marked bullet while Juliette positions herself in front of a bullseye target, one hand on her hip and her smile still unwavering.

One of the most dangerous stunts known to mankind…

I push my way forward in the crowd, cursing myself for arriving so late. I can't let her go through with this. People have died (*will* die, from the viewpoint of this era) when this trick went wrong. And if there's someone out there, someone associated with TUB, who's *trying* to kill Juliette, well, this would be the perfect opportunity. All it'd take is a bit of sabotage: a squib load or swapping the blanks for live rounds. I press forward, ignoring the irritated looks shot my direction. This is what I'm here for: to protect her.

The Amazing Velés loads the pistol and raises it, pointed directly at Juliette's outturned palm. I find a burst of speed and accidentally knock over a man with a cane.

"Hey! Watch where you're going!"

I don't respond. I can't. I'm nearly at the edge of the stage.

"Stop! Don't do it!" I yell, but amid the excited crowd's countdown, my voice is lost.

"Five… four… three…"

I look around. What should I do? What *can* I do?

"Two… one…"

Ignoring the protests of those around me, I hoist myself up on the stage. The pistol lets out a deafening *crack*, and I fling myself at Juliette, knocking her to the ground. I land on top of her in a flurry of red feathers and curls.

"Chandler?" She grabs onto her slipping wig. "What are you doing?"

"Close the curtain! Close the curtain!" the Amazing Velés demands. His face turns a bright red as he looks out on the crowd, whose cheers have warped into a noisy mixture of laughter and booing. He's frozen in place, obviously horrified and uncertain what to do with my unexpected interruption.

"Get off." Juliette shoves me with one hand while straightening her wig with the other. She faces the crowd, smoothing down the ruffled feathers of her skirt and beaming out at them with her brilliant smile.

"Ladies and gentlemen," she announces. At her words, the crowd falls silent. "As you see, not everyone trusts my skill as much as the Amazing Velés does."

Chuckles and grumbles ripple throughout the crowd, and I groan at being the butt of the joke. I'm pretty sure when Dr. Wells sent me back here to keep her safe, this wasn't what he had in mind.

"However, even with the interference of my dashing knight in shining armor—" She pauses here for the crowd to laugh appreciatively. "—I still managed to pluck the bullet from the air." She holds up a small, silvery object for the crowd to see, and immediately, their grumblings turn to applause. The Amazing Velés sidles up beside her and grabs her arm, holding the bullet higher. He seems to have overcome his shock and closes the show as if nothing's wrong.

I, meanwhile, receive a nudge in the ribs with the toe of someone's boot. From behind the curtain, the obscured figure hisses, "Get off the stage, you idiot!"

Groaning, I roll to my knees. A wrinkled hand shoots out from backstage, grabs me by the shoulder, and—as the magician and his assistant bow and the audience's applause roars—pulls me from the stage.

CHAPTER SIX

I sit on a crate backstage, my head in his hands, trying to sort out what I'm going to tell the Amazing Velés, and how I expect to get a job from him now, after such a rocky introduction. It's not the *worst* situation I've ever gotten myself into—at least I'm not tied up, unconscious, on a space colony that's about to explode—but when Juliette ducks behind the curtain and whispers, "What were you thinking?" I somehow feel worse than I did then.

"I don't know. I just… It's a dangerous trick. I don't think you should do it."

"He fires a blank," Juliette says incredulously. "You didn't honestly believe I was catching it, did you?"

"No, but—"

"And what business is it of yours which tricks we do? Who do you think you are, anyway?"

Raised voices approaching from the side of the stage interrupt our conversation, for which I'm grateful. There was no way I was going to come up with a satisfying answer to that question without showing all my cards.

When the Amazing Velés strides in from around the corner, followed by the gray-haired man who'd pulled me backstage, I rise to my feet.

"What's the meaning of this?" the magician asks. His face is still flushed, and he pulls off his gloves and his jacket as he speaks and slaps them down on a trunk. "Juliette, who is this idiot?"

Juliette opens her mouth, looks over at me, and sighs. "His name is Chandler. We met earlier today at the fair. He's harmless, Viggo. Just a little… overenthusiastic."

I'd prefer descriptors like "heroic" or "brave," but I suppose "harmless" and "overenthusiastic" will have to do for now. At least I'm not "unwelcome" or "creepy."

"I ought to have you driven out of town for causing such an uproar. And you—" He turns to Juliette. "What on earth were you thinking, running your mouth like that on stage? What did I tell you? The assistant is *silent.*"

"You seemed flustered," she says, obviously taken aback by his criticism. "I was trying to help."

"That's not your job."

"Well, technically—" I start.

"You. Enough." Viggo turns on me, his face reddening. "I ought to—"

"Now, now, Viggo." The gray-haired man, who's been watching the whole scene with a frown, steps between us. "I'm sure the gentleman meant well. You think if he intended harm he'd still be sitting here?"

"He ruined the finale, Father."

"He caused a scene, that's true, but what have I always taught you? The show must go on. No one was harmed, and frankly, I think it added a bit more excitement to the final trick. An element of surprise. A heightened sense of tension."

"Thank you, Mr. Velés." Juliette turns to me with a look of profound weariness. "I think it's best if you—"

"—come with you." My interruption startles everyone, most of all me. The others gape, and Viggo is the first to respond.

"Come with us? Are you mad? You ruined my show and now you want… what? A job? So you can bother Juliette further?"

"Yes. That is, no. I don't have any intention of bothering Juliette. Or anyone else. But I do want a job." The conversation isn't going quite as I'd hoped, but I turn up the charm anyway, flashing a smile as if I know what I'm doing.

Confession: I rarely ever know what I'm doing.

"Obviously you need some better security," I say, "someone to watch the crowd and make sure no one else interferes with the show like I, regrettably, did this evening. Your magic is simply too convincing; I thought the lady was in danger. I know now that there was nothing to fear, but you take this show on the road, and surely I won't be the only gentleman who tries to leap to the lady's rescue."

Juliette opens her mouth as if to protest, and Viggo lets out a cry of disbelief, but the gray-haired man places his hand on his son's shoulder. "He's right. Imogene was a fine assistant, but you must admit, she wasn't nearly as convincing as Juliette. You saw the pull she has on the audience—the gentlemen in particular. You're busy onstage, Viggo, and I must remain behind the curtain to ensure everything runs smoothly; it may be wise to have a man out front with his eyes on the crowd to make sure no one oversteps their bounds, especially if we're going to bring the show to larger cities. Besides, we could use another set of muscles around here for moving the equipment around. Give these old bones a rest."

"Then we'll hire a laborer," Viggo says between clenched teeth. "Someone *else*. Just look at his hands; this man's never worked a day in his life."

I've honestly never paid much attention to my hands, but as I look at them now, still scraped and raw from climbing the tree trunk, I have to admit that Viggo has a point. I do most of my work at a computer—my fingers flying through holographic projections—not as a laborer. Growing up, my hands had a worn, hardened look from climbing real rocks, riding real bikes, and building things, but when was the last time I'd had so much as a blister? With so many things—including exercise, work, and recreation—automated, is it possible the 22nd century has made me weak?

"I'm stronger than I look," I insist. "Let me prove it."

"You should've seen him in the pole-climbing competition this afternoon," Juliette says. I shoot her a grateful smile. I don't know why she's taking my side, but I'm glad.

"Did he win?" Viggo taps the toe of his shining black shoe.

Juliette glances at me, her eyes wide as if she's suddenly realized her mistake in bringing it up.

"Almost." I meet Juliette's eye. I won't tell her secret.

Her lips curl up in a tiny smile that quickens my pulse.

"Then it's settled," the older Mr. Velés says. "You're hired. You'll be provided room and board—such as it is on the road—and five percent of the show's earnings. Do a good job and in a few months, we'll see if we can increase that."

"Father," Viggo hisses. His displeasure at the arrangement is obvious, and I can't help feeling a bit smug. "Don't you think we ought to discuss this first?"

"My mind is made up," Mr. Velés says.

"But five percent?"

"It's not your concern how I spend my money." He turns to me. "Come this way, and I'll show you the wagon where you'll be staying."

I move to go, but Viggo catches my arm. The magician leans in, his breath hot in my ear and his nails digging into my skin. "Stay away from Juliette. She doesn't need a man like you skulking around."

I smile as I pry his fingers from my arm, then turn and wave to Juliette before following the old man from the stage.

That night, I lie in my designated bunk as Mr. Velés snores on the mattress below. It's harder to fall asleep here than I expected. Apparently, I've gotten used to ambient white noise humming from my ergonomic bed's speakers and my climate controls being set to exactly the ideal temperature and humidity for a good night's sleep.

Our wagon is larger than Juliette's, but it seems much less roomy, due to the narrow bunk beds on either side. It hardly has space for a small table, and locked trunks sit at the foot of each bed. When asked if I'd be bringing along any personal possessions, I merely smiled and assured Mr. Velés that I traveled light.

Outside the tent, Viggo's dog barks.

"Shut up, Brutus." I recognize Viggo's voice approaching, though it sounds somewhat less refined and steady than when he was on stage. He's probably been out enjoying one of the small town's numerous drinking establishments. Good ole' Midwest.

The dog barks again, then something makes a *thump*ing noise and the dog whines. "Don't wake the old man."

"The Amazing Velés," a second male voice says, chortling, "traveling the country with his old man."

"Shut up, Harrison. It's not like I had a choice."

"No, no, of course not. Not much you can do when the old man's the one holding the purse strings. You'd better ask for an allowance next time you're in town, though. I'm not paying for your drinks again."

I close my eyes as the footsteps approach, feigning sleep.

"Next time I'm in town," Viggo says, "I'll be a rich man. One way or another."

"Right. And that fine young assistant will be sharing more with you than just the stage, am I right?"

The other man's crude laughter fades into the distance as the canvas flap of the wagon slaps open. Viggo stumbles about the small space for a few moments as he pulls off his shirt, and then he collapses into the opposite bunk. He's snoring long before my fists unclench and my pulse slows back down to normal.

CHAPTER SEVEN

Mr. Velés puts me to work immediately the next morning, hauling equipment back and forth, standing guard at the corner of the stage during each performance, and cleaning up afterward. When Juliette performs the bullet catch, I watch obediently from the side of the stage, though my heart leaps at the sound of the pistol firing.

The manual labor is exhausting work, using all sorts of muscles that somehow are overlooked by my gym's automated training equipment, and it doesn't take long for my palms to become scraped and chapped. A few more days of this, and I'll have some nice calluses.

As we gather for dinner the evening of that first day, I'm distracted by thoughts of how nice it'd be to collapse into my bunk and sleep solidly until the morning.

Juliette, however, is a bit of a night owl.

The four of us dine together on some sort of vegetable stew that's somehow both too hot and too cold at the same time, with barely a word exchanged between us. Afterward, Juliette sneaks out of sight and into the darkness. Before I can follow, Viggo throws an arm around my shoulder and holds out his bowl.

"Where do you think you're off to? Don't you know the rules?

The newcomer's in charge of washing up."

I look to Mr. Velés for confirmation, but he's already leaning back with his feet propped up on a wooden crate. His hands are crossed over his chest and his eyes are closed.

The next day, I get a jump on him. As soon as the bowls are empty, I swoop in with an elegant bow, gather them up while everyone else is still seated, and rush them to the washbasin which I've already filled with boiled water prior to sitting down to eat.

"Nice to see someone take initiative around here," Mr. Velés says as he lights his pipe. Over the wisps of smoke, Viggo glares at me.

Me, I'm still scrubbing as fast as I can so that, by the time Juliette stands, clears her throat, and excuses herself, all I have to do is wipe my hands on my towel, leave the heavy iron pot soaking, and sneak away after her.

Out past the supply wagons, I lose sight of her. If we were in the 22nd century, I'd head for the nearest data port, hack into the GPS of her personal vision device, and track her that way, but things are more complicated here. Without data ports or personal vision devices, I'm left to stand there, looking lost like an idiot.

"Are you following me?" She steps out from behind a shed.

"Yes?" I try to smile, but I know how this looks. I look obsessed. "Just wondering if you'd like company."

I don't know what I'll do if she says no. I care about her safety because it's my job. It's what I've come here for. But I've found that I also care what she thinks of me, and I don't want her to think I'm a stalker.

She stares at me, her hands on her hips, obviously trying to decide whether she can trust me. Whether I'm a stalker.

"I'm not a stalker."

"Stalker?" She raises her brows at what must be an anachronistic slip-up.

"Harasser. Prowler. Creep." I shake my head; that sounds too modern, too. "Look, I'm your bodyguard, right? So it's my job to make sure you're safe—onstage and off."

She slowly nods. "All right."

And that's how our evening outings begin.

As the weeks pass, our walks along the shores of Saginaw Bay quickly become my favorite time of day. Each evening after dinner, Juliette bundles up against the lake's chill and together we walk the beach as she recounts her idyllic childhood in rural Ohio, her decision to join up with her childhood friend and his father on their tour of the country, and the latest adventures of her day—and there are always adventures.

"Today during rehearsals, I accidentally set Viggo's silk scarf on fire," she says with a laugh that bursts from her like sunshine. She readjusts her own scarf over her head as a gust of wind threatens to yank it free. "You should've seen his face. He couldn't decide whether to be frightened or angry."

"I suspect he feels that way rather often," I mutter.

"He's really not that bad once you get to know him," she insists.

"Right," I say, then fall silent, hoping she'll fill in the gaps, give me some clue about the extent of their relationship. His interest is obvious, at least to me, but Juliette's feelings toward him are harder to read. Not that it's any of my business, I suppose. It's not like *I* have a shot with her; we're from different eras, and eventually, I'm going to have to return to mine and leave her here. I kick a stone toward the lake.

"He just takes this show so seriously," she says. "He's always had lofty ambitions, and he works so hard toward them that you can't help but to admire his gumption."

I can, though I didn't say so.

"At any rate," she continues, "he sent me to the storage wagon to fetch him a new scarf, and I found this."

She holds out a book and I take it in my hands, squinting to see its contents in the moonlight. It's handwritten, and at first, I assume it's a journal, but as I page through, I see that it is, in fact, an instruction booklet of some sort, with all sorts of equations and diagrams and sketches that seem too technologically advanced for this era.

"I picked it up thinking that it was a record of magic tricks. Mr. Velés's, perhaps. Or his father's before him; I heard he was a magician as well." Juliette leans in toward the journal, and I catch a whiff of her lavender scent. "I was hoping to find some new trick to use for the finale—"

"Instead of the bullet catch?" I ask in surprise.

I haven't told her, but in the process of deconstructing the stage between towns, I'd discovered a bullet hole through the center of the bull's eye target where she'd been standing for the trick. Viggo had scoffed and accused me of planting the "evidence" myself, and even Mr. Velés couldn't say for sure that the hole hadn't been there for weeks, months, or years.

"We can't discontinue the trick without something just as impressive to replace it," Mr. Velés had told me, firmly putting an end to the conversation.

Since then, I've personally inspected the ivory-handled pistol the Amazing Velés uses for the finale before each show, ensuring that the chambers are clean and that only blanks are stored with it. The "Amazing" Velés probably won't be pleased if he finds out I've been poking around his props, but I can't shake the feeling that this is just the sort of opportunity TUB would take advantage of.

Juliette shrugs and stares out at the waves. "I've been thinking about what you said. The trick does seem rather dangerous, particularly if someone was trying to cause trouble."

"You think someone might be trying to cause trouble?"

"Oh, don't make a fuss." She laughs and waves me off, but I can tell by the set of her shoulders that she's not entirely at ease. "Since you mentioned it the other day, I've been paying close attention. Yesterday, I discovered someone—a stranger—backstage before our first show, looking at the trick box that Viggo uses to cut me in half."

Someone backstage? TUB? Or just an admirer hoping for a closer look?

"What did they look like?" I ask. "Why didn't you say something?"

"He ran off before I could get a good look. I didn't even think about it until later, during the show. There's a little mechanism that pushes the false feet through the bottom of the box that I have to kick out before pulling myself up into the upper two portions of the box. But the mechanism stuck. I couldn't get the false feet to pop out. I barely got out of the way before Viggo cut through with that first saw." She hesitates, sneaking glances at me and obviously trying to gauge my reaction.

Being sawed in half would be an awful way to go, and the thought of someone doing that to Juliette makes me want to punch something. Or someone.

"I think you're right," she says. "I think someone is trying to ruin the Amazing Velés' show."

"Ruin his show?" I turn to face her. "Don't you see? Someone's trying to harm *you*."

Juliette waves the notion away. "Who would try to harm me? I don't know anyone here. I don't know anyone at all who'd have any reason to hold a grudge. Whereas Viggo... Well, he's not the most personable man. No, he's gotten on someone's bad side, and now they're trying to destroy his reputation. I just know it. Another magician, perhaps. In fact, no, I'm certain of it. It's the only logical explanation."

My molars grind against one another. I've been too lax, too afraid of being found out or staying in Juliette's good graces when what I really ought to have been worried about was her physical well-being. I've forgotten my real purpose here. After all, if Juliette dies now, there's no Elise, and without Elise, my past is messed up in the most paradoxical manner possible.

But what can I do? Juliette won't quit the show; that much is clear. Ever since her parents passed away, she's been determined to learn the business so that she can someday fly on the trapeze. Besides, what would that do to history? Dr. Wells didn't tell me a thing about Juliette's life after this summer except the implication that she'll go on to become Elise's great-great-grandmother somehow. What if she needs to follow the Amazing Velés's show to meet Elise's great-great-grandfather, whoever the lucky guy will be?

A horrible thought crosses my mind. It better not be Viggo. The two may have been childhood friends, but I can't bear the thought of Juliette marrying that creep. Why hadn't I thought to look at the surnames on those genealogy pages Dr. Wells had waved around? I guess it hadn't seemed important at the time, back when Juliette was just someone who'd lived long ago. Before I knew her.

"But look." Juliette reaches over to the book, which I'd forgotten I was still holding. She flips quickly through it until finally, she lands on a page near the back. "Here. I've read a bit, and I don't think the journal is about magic at all. It's about traveling through time! Can you even imagine? Time travel! It's not real, of course… It can't be, but what if it were? Wouldn't that be amazing?"

I lean in closer, certain that what I'm was seeing in the dim moonlight must be my imagination. There, sketched out in bold lines, with a cutout on one page and all the important inner parts labeled, is a spitting image of the Wormhole Device that's tucked away in my pocket.

CHAPTER EIGHT

It's only a short wagon ride to the show's next stop. Even in these few weeks, I've grown to resent the days of setting up and taking down the stage with its hidden panels and trap doors, not because of the work itself—which, admittedly, has rubbed my palms raw—but because it involves spending time away from Juliette. If that wasn't bad enough, I also have to be in the company of Viggo, whose father insists he help with the manual labor.

"You boys are getting faster at this," Juliette says, balancing a lunch tray on her hip. "Are you sure I can't help?"

"Those rye sandwiches and lemonade are plenty help," I say with a smile. It'd been a long time since I had anything but Punch-In back home; I'd nearly forgotten how good made-from-scratch food could be. "Thank you."

"Yes, thank you." Viggo grabs a sandwich and winks at Juliette. "I always enjoy something sweet with my lunch."

Juliette rolls her eyes, but not before a smile reaches her lips. "The lemonade was a gift from the farmer three stalls down; I'll be sure to tell him how much you appreciate it." She turns to me. "I'm afraid I've bent my last mending needle. Would you mind walking into town with me this afternoon to purchase a new one?"

"Of course," Viggo interrupts, his mouth still full. He sets aside his sandwich and takes her arm. "Why don't we go now?"

"I…" Juliette looks up in what appears to be genuine confusion.

"I believe the lady was speaking to me," I say.

"Nonsense. You have far too much to do here in setting up this stage."

"Juliette?" I ask. As much as I don't want her to spend the afternoon with Viggo—how am I supposed to keep her safe then?—I won't force my company on her.

"I assumed you'd want to spend the afternoon practicing the show," she tells him.

"Nah." He straightens his hat. "I can take one afternoon off to walk you into town."

She looks at me apologetically and shrugs. "It looks like Viggo will walk me to town."

I bite my tongue and try to smile. "Don't stay out too late, you two."

"We'll be back in time for dinner," she promises, and I know she heard my underlying request: I'd still like to have our evening walk.

As the two start down the dirt road, Juliette's laughter—high and light—takes a long time to fade into the distance, and even then, I keep looking up from time to time, thinking I've heard her return.

Without Viggo's help, construction takes longer than usual, and with each passing hour, I'm more and more convinced that I was an idiot to let them up and leave like that. It's like sending a jackal to protect a sheep from the wolves. Though, no, that analogy doesn't work because Juliette's no sheep. Still, what was I supposed to do? I couldn't just shirk my duties.

By the time I finish constructing the stage, I'm hot and sore and tired and irritable. It's nearly time for dinner, and I ought to wash up, but I haven't seen Viggo or Juliette return. When the sun dips low on the flat horizon, I pace outside the wagons, my gaze constantly flicking back to the fence opening that serves as the fairgrounds' entrance. They've got to be returning any moment. Darkness falls with no sign of them, and finally, I can't hold still any longer. I pat my pocket to ensure that the Wormhole Device is still safely tucked away and set off in the darkness toward town.

I wish I had my personal vision device with its night vision settings. At this point, I'd even settle for a good old-fashioned flashlight. The road's uneven and I shuffle along slowly to ensure I don't trip over a rock or a log or a sleeping grizzly. Do they have grizzlies here? I don't even know. Now's probably not the best time to start thinking along those lines.

In the distance, coyotes howl and other nighttime creatures wake from their warm daytime slumber. Crickets, owls… I can't remember the last time I heard the night so full of life. And the stars! They remind me of the flight of the *Continuum*'s escape pod, with the galaxy whizzing past, looking almost near enough to touch.

I don't pass any grizzlies or anything else on the road, and when I arrive on the downtown streets, bright lantern light points to the few establishments open this late. I choose the first one—a tavern of some sort—and duck inside.

The establishment is small and noisy, filled with chatter and upbeat music played on a pipe organ. I scan the crowd, craning my neck to spot Juliette's coiffed hairdo or Viggo's slick black top hat.

I find them sitting in a corner booth with a man whose back is to me. Juliette leans in, her face bright with excitement, while Viggo fiddles with the empty glass before him, running his finger along the rim and looking utterly bored.

"Chandler!" Juliette waves, gesturing me to join them at the table. "You absolutely *must* meet this man. He's a scientist, and we've been discussing time travel, and he has the most fascinating ideas! Dr. Wells, this is Chandler. Chandler, I'd like you to meet Dr. Wells."

I can't stop staring. I mindlessly swig one glass of whiskey, then another. I'm so engrossed in studying the man across the table that I barely even taste the sharp liquor.

Dr. Wells is younger than I've ever seen him—with salt-and-pepper hair and fewer pounds on him—and shows no indication of recognizing me at all. That shouldn't come as a surprise. After all, this Dr. Wells obviously predates the one I met in 2012 when I worked for TUB. But by how much? How much younger is this doctor? He must've discovered time travel already for him to be here, but has he established his time travel agency yet? Has he hired Elise? And more importantly, does he know that it's Elise's great-great-grandmother who's currently sitting across from him, asking question after question about the time-space continuum and paradoxes and scientific theories which at this point in history have no name?

"What about you, Chandler?" Juliette asks, pulling me out of my musings. "Would you rather travel to the past or to the future?"

"Hypothetically, of course," Dr. Wells adds.

"Right. Hypothetically." I eye Dr. Wells, searching for some flicker of acknowledgment, some hint that he knows—somehow—who I am, but the older man is inscrutable. "Hypothetically, I think I'd like to travel to the future."

"Really? Why?" Juliette asks.

I run my finger along the grain of the table. How can I possibly explain to her what a beautiful place the future is, without giving away what I know about it? "It's... still full of possibilities."

"So is the present," Juliette insists, gesturing around to the dim tavern, to all the people around us. "Everyone sitting here is full of potential."

"I suppose," I say, then try again. "In the future, anything could happen. Anything could be invented, discovered, explored. And the technology! We can't even imagine today what things might be possible a hundred or two hundred years from now. Space travel. Communications. Computers."

"Computers?" Dr. Wells looks up from his ale, startled.

Juliette glances from me to him, and I can almost see the questions forming in her mind. I bite back a curse at the booze that's loosened my tongue and muddled my brain. Dr. Wells ought to add another Rule to his list: "Don't drink and time travel."

I smile at my own joke, and it's only when Juliette asks me to repeat myself that I realize I've spoken aloud.

"Where are you from again?" Dr. Wells asks, his brow furrowing.

"Chicago," I say, which is mostly true. It's where I grew up, though I haven't set foot there in a decade, outside the occasional layover.

"Fascinating…" Dr. Wells says. "I'm from New York myself. Tell me… how old were you at the time of the fire?"

I open my mouth, but nothing comes out. This is 1893, but what year was the fire? Sometime in the 1870s? Recalling historical dates has never been one of my strengths, even when I haven't been drinking. What am I supposed to do now?

Thinking fast, I spin to face Juliette, allowing my elbow to knock against my half-empty glass. Viggo lets out a shout of dismay and leaps up as the whiskey cascades into his lap.

"You clumsy fool!" Viggo, who'd been dulled to a silent stupor during our conversation, dabs at his shirt with a napkin.

"I'm sorry, old sport," I say, for some reason channeling Jay Gatsby before realizing I'm decades ahead of that era still. "You ought to soak it before it stains."

"I'm so sorry, doctor." Juliette rises to her feet and shoots Viggo and me a scowl. "It seems we ought to be headed back."

"Yes, yes." Dr. Wells nods. "I understand."

"Come on, Juliette." Viggo brushes past me and heads to the door. She sighs and offers Dr. Wells another apology before following.

I try to follow, but as I pass his seat, Dr. Wells catches my arm. "Just a moment, young man. Tell me, now that they're gone: *When* are you from?"

CHAPTER NINE

I struggle to find words to respond. "I don't think I ought to..."

"Of course," Dr. Wells says, looking around. "Not here. Can I meet you tomorrow? After the magic show?"

"Sure." As soon as the word is out of my mouth, I regret it, but as Juliette and Viggo disappear through the door and out into the night, I can't think of anything else to do but tip my head to Dr. Wells and rush out after them.

The hours leading up to our rendezvous are agonizing. My time-travel training with TUB was rudimentary, focused almost entirely on the practical aspects of how to survive and blend in within a future era. When Elise came to Retrieve me in 2112, all I cared about was staying there, protecting my own life, and making sure Dodge was cared for. I realize now, as I try to sort out what exactly I'm going to tell Dr. Wells, what a tough spot that must've put her in.

Surely there's danger in telling him too much. One wrong word, and I could destroy my own timeline, making it so that Dr. Wells doesn't start his travel agency, doesn't hire Elise, doesn't send her forward in time to Retrieve me. On the other hand, I sure could use an ally, particularly since Viggo seems all too willing to place Juliette in increasingly dangerous situations. One thing's clear: I need to tread carefully.

I'm still ruminating over all this, watching the crowd gather for the final show of the day, when a pair of dirty-faced delivery boys rush up the road with an enormous crate on a dolly. I intercept them as they're trying to haul it up a ramp to the platform backstage.

"Hey! You! What is this?"

"Delivery for the Amazing Velés," one of the boys says, sticking out his hand for a tip. I drop a few coins into it, and the boys rush away. I circle the crate, but there are no markings on it, nothing to indicate what might be inside. Only one way to find out. I pick up a crowbar and begin to pry it open.

"Ah! My delivery's arrived." Viggo saunters up from offstage, already wearing his shining black suit and top hat. "Quickly, haul it over here, just behind the curtain."

I'd nearly gotten one side of the crate open, but I set down the crowbar and—with a bit of direction from Viggo—haul it to the indicated spot.

"What is it?" I ask, crossing my arms, trying to look threatening, yet not *too* threatening. It's a fine balance to strike.

"A surprise for Juliette." Viggo grins widely, ignoring my posturing entirely. He ducks behind the stage's curtain. "Juliette! Come here and see!"

Juliette, who from the looks of it was just mending a few broken feathers from her headdress, glances questioningly from Viggo to me. "What is it?"

"Our newest act," Viggo says, throwing his arms out in a flourish of bravado, even though there's only the three of us to see. He pulls the side of the crate open to reveal its contents.

"It's a... what is it?" Juliette asks.

"It's a water tank." The magician circles the object, prying the rest of the crate away. "For our escape act."

"Underwater?" Juliette asks, her eyes lighting up. "Oh, how exciting!"

Her eager expression makes my stomach drop. "Don't you think that's dangerous?"

"That's the whole point." She stands on her tiptoes to examine it.

"The old man's lined us up some shows near Chicago later this summer," Viggo tells her. "If we're going to compete with the acts offered at the World's Fair, we'll need some more daring tricks."

"I wish we could perform at the fair," Juliette muses, running her fingers along the glass.

"Yes, well… if I were in charge, we would be." Viggo tosses the crowbar aside. "That's the problem with the old man; he wants to continue doing things the old way. Frightened to try anything new." At this, he shoots me a disgusted glance, one that loosens my tongue.

"Dangerous isn't always exciting. Sometimes it's just dangerous," I say, frowning at the tank. Each of the four sides is made of glass, held together by a metal framework. On the top, a wooden lid is held down by a series of locks.

"It's precisely the same as the act we've been doing," Viggo says, "but instead of being locked in a trunk, my lovely assistant will be locked in here."

"And your father bought this… contraption for this act?" Juliette's brow furrows.

"It was a gift," Viggo says, "from an investor."

"An investor?" I ask. My gut tells me something's definitely not right here. "Does your show often attract investors?"

"Of course it does," Viggo snaps. "Not that it's any of your concern."

Juliette twirls a feather between her fingers and stares up at the glass. "Does your father know?" she asks pointedly.

"Go finish getting dressed." Viggo shakes the dust from his cloak.

"The lady asked you a question," I say, unable to hold back my irritation any longer. I blink, and my fist is closed around his collar.

"Chandler," Juliette scolds, stepping between us. "This is between Viggo and me. You're not helping matters. Viggo, tell me honestly.

Does your father know about this device?"

"Never mind my father." Viggo spits and throws his cloak over his shoulder. "Or this gibface. They're stuck in the past, both of them, and the day is coming when they won't be able to follow us around, sticking their noses in the everyday workings of the business. It's my job to make sure the show will continue when my father's gone, and to do that, we need to embrace the future. No one wants to see safe little parlor tricks anymore. This is the age of electricity, of mechanical wonders. Just look at what a show Ferris is making of that giant wheel of his down in Chicago. Would people be so impressed if there weren't an element of risk, of excitement and thrill? No, mark my words: this is an era of danger, and *that* is what will set the Amazing Velés apart."

Viggo's words echo in my skull as I watch the magician perform his act. The edge of the stage digs into my spine as I lean back, trying to get a better view of the crowd. Saginaw's a larger city than the others we've been to thus far, and the crowd here is boisterous. Some have undoubtedly already been sampling the products of the city's breweries, despite it only being early afternoon.

Just before the show began, I caught a glimpse of Dr. Wells, wandering on the edges of the crowd with a large, colorful lollipop in his hand. He caught my eye and tipped the candied sweet in greeting but didn't approach.

Now, my mind's torn between thoughts of Viggo, Juliette, and him. What *was* the old man doing in this era anyway?

Onstage, Juliette assists Viggo with a card trick—the latter barely managing to mask his disdain for the "safe little parlor trick." Juliette, on the other hand, beams and flourishes each card with such enthusiasm that the audience doesn't even seem to notice the bored edge in the Amazing Velés's voice.

The next trick is supposed to be the trunk escape, but instead of dragging out the heavy trunk, Viggo stands before an empty stage, a sly smile upon his face. My hatred for him reaches a boiling point— 212 degrees of pure loathing—because even before he speaks, I have a sneaking suspicion of what he's up to. And if he tries, I swear I'll jump right up on that stage and strangle him.

Juliette looks around him pointedly—her smile never breaking— but he doesn't acknowledge her. *Coward.*

"Our next trick is a test of daring… a dangerous escape from certain death. Only the bravest and most skilled would dare test themselves in such a way. Yet today, that is just what you will see here. I give to you… the underwater escape!"

The curtain whips open and the tank is revealed, filled with clear, crisp water.

I nearly leap to the stage right then, except that Juliette is already gliding over to Viggo and whispering something to him, her smiling lips barely moving. I take a breath. Let her try to work it out with him. He whispers something back in a tense growl, something that sounds like, "Of course I inspected it."

She shakes her head definitively.

"Fine. Then I'll do it." He turns to the crowd and raises his voice. "Yes, ladies and gentlemen! I, the Amazing Velés, will escape from this underwater prison."

I take a step back and cross my arms over my chest. Doing the trick without any practice in the tank is an idiotic idea all around, but I have no loyalty to Viggo, and as long as he doesn't put Juliette in harm's way, he can do whatever dunder-headed thing he wants. Besides, according to Juliette, Viggo was the one to teach her the escape tricks; he ought to be fine.

Unless… Unless there was more to this mysterious "investor" of his.

Juliette beams out at the crowd, but I'm close enough to see how her hands shake as she snaps the locks shut around Viggo's handcuffs and see her lips move, obviously trying to talk him out of this sudden change of plans. A pang of something sharp and sour cuts through me as their hands touch, and I look away. Mr. Velés is nowhere to be seen, which I find rather suspicious. Surely he'd step in and tell his son this was a bad idea.

I glance around, trying to see if there's anyone who appears out of place, or out of their proper time.

Bound in a set of chains, with handcuffs around each wrist, Viggo climbs a stepladder to the top of the tank, while going on and on about what a dangerous act this is and telling anyone who felt faint of heart to please excuse themselves from the audience. Then, he steps off the ladder and into the tank with barely a splash, and Juliette carefully snaps the cover into place.

I turn my back to the stage and face the crowd, more interested in watching their reactions than in the spectacle Viggo's making. The crowd is collectively curious, tense, nervous, and amused, smiling and laughing as though watching the magician struggle against his bonds underwater is some sort of great joke. Over the floral bonnet of a plain-looking woman, a man catches my eye. His mouth is bent down in a frown, and—as I watch—he raises his arm to his face. His lips move, as if he's speaking to someone, but no one nearby seems to acknowledge him.

Then I notice his watch.

He's wearing a thick black wristwatch with a shining band. This, though, I know isn't just any watch. It's a recording device as well. I had one just like it once, given to me by none other than TUB.

"Out of the way!" I try to push my way through the crowd, fighting not to lose sight of the man, but a commotion onstage draws my attention away.

"Someone help!" a voice calls from the crowd. "He's drowning!"

I glance over my shoulder to where Juliette stands atop the ladder, frantically trying to pry open the lid. Beneath her, Viggo floats, his arms still bound in their restraints and an expression of pure panic on his submerged face.

CHAPTER TEN

The Amazing Velés is dead.

I sit on a wooden crate outside the wagon. Juliette's weeping rips through the thin canvas covering, puncturing my heart over and over. This is wrong. It wasn't supposed to happen like this. Dr. Wells told me that Juliette spent the summer traveling with the Amazing Velés, but now the magician is dead. What's she going to do now? What am *I* going to do?

I whirl around at the sound of footsteps approaching the canvas flap. Instead of Juliette, though, it's Mr. Velés, looking pale and worn and ten years older than this morning. He sits down heavily on a crate beside me and takes in a long drag from his pipe.

"I'm sorry." The words cascade from my mouth. "This is my fault. I should have—"

The old man holds up a hand to stop me. "No. There's no one to blame but Viggo himself. He acted recklessly, performing that trick on stage without properly checking all of his equipment."

"What do you mean?" My body tenses.

"The lock stuck. The key went in but the tumbler wouldn't turn. That's why he couldn't get out." His voice cracks.

I feel ill. It was supposed to have been Juliette in there struggling to free herself from that tank. I bury my head in my hands. Knowing everything I'd known about TUB and their plans, I shouldn't have let Viggo do the trick. I should have stopped him.

But I'd failed. TUB may not have gotten exactly what they wanted, but they'd still managed to mess everything up. What good had I done here, anyway? What had Dr. Wells expected me to do?

"Do you know where the tank came from?" I ask quietly.

Mr. Velés rises to his feet. "No, but if I ever find out where he got a box with such shoddy craftsmanship… with a faulty lock…" He looks away, letting the rest of the sentence hang in midair.

When I wake with the glare of an LED light shining in my eyes, I think I'm back in the future somehow, except for some reason my sensory deprivation bed has malfunctioned, so instead of emerging peacefully from sleep to a gradual increase in lighting, my bed is shaking and someone's hissing, "Get up, son!"

My eyes shoot open.

I'm not in my bed. Not even close. I'm lying in a bedroll on the ground outside Juliette's wagon with Dr. Wells crouching over me, an anachronistic flashlight in hand. Suddenly, it all comes back to me—I parked myself here partially because I didn't want to sleep in the same wagon as Viggo's dead body, but mostly because it was the only thing I could think of to do to protect Juliette from the TUB agent, wherever he's lurking.

"Let's go for a walk," Dr. Wells says.

I roll out of my blankets, shivering against the biting wind that whips through the fairgrounds like a restless ghost. Maybe it's Viggo, come back to haunt me. He ought to be haunting the underhanded TUB agent who provided him with the murder-in-a-box.

Once we're out of earshot of the wagons, Dr. Wells speaks up. "Did you have anything to do with that tragedy up there on the stage today?"

Coming from anyone else, I'd have denied it immediately, but Dr. Wells is here from the future, too. There's no use lying to a man with a time machine.

"Indirectly," I say, wondering how to explain the twisted history of how I came to be here, in this late 19th century Midwestern town, trying to protect the great-great-grandmother of a woman I'd once spent two days with in the year 2112. How it's my fault that TUB is trying to snuff Elise out of existence in the first place.

Dr. Wells nods. The darkness hides his expression. "Am I correct in thinking that I know you at some point in my future?"

"Yes."

"And… did I send you here?"

"Afraid so."

Dr. Wells falls silent, and I can tell that he, too, is trying to puzzle out how much foreknowledge he ought to have about his own future, how much information is safe for me to reveal.

"Do you mind if I ask what *you're* doing here?" I ask.

"I'm looking for a way back."

"A way back?"

"Yes, to the future. I'm on a search for the inventor of time travel."

"You mean… you didn't invent it?"

"No, no. I've been standing on the shoulders of one far greater than me," Dr. Wells says, his voice distant and almost sad. "Using his work to shape and direct my own."

"Well, who invented it then?"

He laughs. "I don't know."

"I'm not sure I follow."

Dr. Wells leans against a fence railing. He looks up and sighs. "The stars really are beautiful here, aren't they? I never see them in the city."

I wait, silent, for the old man to gather his thoughts.

Finally, he continues. "When I was younger, I was fascinated with the concept of time travel. Obsessed, one might say. As I grew, I studied physics and mathematics, all with the goal in mind of someday making my own time traveling device."

I lean against the fence and stare up at the stars. One thing the old man is right about: they are beautiful here.

"I studied everything I could get my hands on—books, journals, anything that might point me in the direction of solving that mystery," Dr. Wells continues. "Though I didn't have any luck until one day a friend at a used book store called me up and asked if I was interested in a very old journal that seemed to be all about the particulars of time travel. Of course, I told him yes and picked it up the very next day. It was a small book, leather cover, with no indication of authorship."

My heart skips. What are the chances that it's the same book Juliette found? There must be some connecting thread, a line between points A and B that would lead the scientist here.

"And that's when I found it," Dr. Wells says. "Calculations, diagrams, figures… everything I'd need to make my dreams a reality, all on those pages. There were essentially two elements: a box that would serve as the initial boost to propel the traveler through time, and a small, handheld device that would tether him to his original era and, when he was done with his travels, pull him back to it. The problem, however, was that the final page of the journal, where the precise figures for the second device should have been written, had been torn out."

"So, you came back here to read the journal before it was damaged?"

"Precisely."

"But if you don't find it, you're stuck here."

"Yes, well." Dr. Wells shrugs. "After spending a decade trying to solve the riddle on my own, I figured, well, I have a time machine. Why not use it?"

I'm so taken aback, I can only stare. The Dr. Wells I met briefly in the year 2012 had been known for his rules and for sticking to them religiously. He'd never have been so reckless as this. What could have happened—what would happen in this man's future—to change that?

"The bookseller said he'd purchased it in a lot of books from an estate," Dr. Wells continues, "which I traced backward, year by year, until I discovered it had once been in the possession of the Amazing Velés. So here I am. And perhaps, since you are in the magician's employ and you realize the importance of my task, you might help me find what I'm searching for. Tell me, have you seen anything like this?"

Sure enough, the journal he pulls out of his jacket pocket, though much older and worn now, its pages warped and water-stained, is the exact same one that is currently tucked away in Juliette's wagon.

CHAPTER ELEVEN

I look for an opportune moment to search Juliette's wagon, but it's long in coming. Without Viggo around and with Mr. Velés and Juliette in mourning, many of the everyday tasks fall upon me. I don't mind lending a hand with feeding the horses who pull the wagons or making sure everyone has fresh water to drink from and bathe in. When the director of the fair approaches me after Viggo's hasty, ill-attended funeral to ask about the other scheduled performances, though, I have no idea how to answer him.

"I'm sorry," Mr. Velés says that evening over his bowl of cold beans. They were warm when I'd set them before him, but he hasn't done more than stir them around with a spoon. "I'm afraid I don't know what we're going to do. I'm too old to perform on stage again, and—although no one doubts that you'd do your best, Juliette— you've only been with us such a short while; I'm afraid we haven't had time to train you to do the tricks on your own."

"I could learn," she says, taking his hand.

"Not in time for our scheduled appearances," he says. "Besides, then who would be the lovely assistant? Many of them require another performer who's in on the trick."

"The fair director said if we don't perform tomorrow he's going to have to ask us to leave," I say quietly. I hate being the bearer of bad news, but what can be done?

Juliette looks to me, and I know she's wondering if I could be trained, but I shake my head. Even if I did have any skill in showmanship—which I don't—I can't focus on keeping her safe if I'm busy trying to coax a rabbit out of a hat.

"I'm afraid we'll have to go our separate ways," Mr. Velés says. "Without a show, I have no income, and with no income, I have no means to pay you. No, I think it's best that I sell all this. It ought to bring in enough for me to live on until I get back on my feet again, find another way to support myself."

Juliette nibbles her thumbnail, and the desperation in her eyes is apparent.

"I've got it." She slaps a hand against her thigh. "We'll go to Chicago."

"Chicago?" Mr. Velés asks. "I don't follow."

Neither do I, but something about the eager look on her face makes me think I won't like what she's suggesting.

"Well, we're not going to find another magician out here. That's for certain," she says, gesturing around wildly. "But a place like Chicago, we'll have far better luck, particularly with the World's Fair going on. We'll put out an ad for a new Amazing Velés, someone who already knows the basics of showmanship and magic so it won't take so long to teach him. Surely anyone with a dream to be a magician would appreciate your knowledge and experience, not to mention your equipment and personal connections."

Mr. Velés begins to shake his head, and she adds, "Or we can change the name, if you'd like. But we have everything else we need; it'd be a shame to see all of this packed up and stowed away, all your knowledge forgotten. Please, just let us try."

The old man sighs and studies his empty palms. "I don't know… I have a colleague down in Flint. I was thinking I might stay with him for a bit until I sort things out."

Juliette will not be deterred. "Then I'll go myself. I'll find a new magician for you and bring him back to Flint. We can pick up the tour again there. Just give me some time. And promise us you won't sell anything until I return."

"You can't do that," I blurt out.

Juliette looks as though she's about to give me a piece of her mind, but Mr. Velés interrupts. "No, my dear. He's right. I can't allow you to go alone; it wouldn't be safe."

"Then come with me." Juliette turns to me, pleading. She quickly adds, "If you're so concerned about my safety."

"Just the two of you?" Mr. Velés frowns. "Without a chaperone? No, that won't do, either."

Juliette's face falls. We all know she has no one to fill that role.

My own thoughts are a muddle, and I'm not sure which side I should be arguing. To protect Juliette, I have to remain near her, but without a new magician, we'll all be forced to go our separate ways, and then what excuse would I have for following her? Mr. Velés was generous in giving me a job with the show; I can't count on such luck next time. It'll be difficult to watch for TUB in such a busy, bustling city like Chicago, but then again, it might be the perfect place to evade the agent. We can blend in with the crowd flocking there to attend the fair. We'll just have to leave here without letting anyone else know where we're going. Though, on second thought, I ought to tell Dr. Wells.

Suddenly, it all seems clear. There's only one thing to do.

"I'll ask my grandfather." As soon as the words are out of my mouth, I realize my slip. Juliette has already met Dr. Wells. Even if I can persuade Dr. Wells to go along with it and convince Mr. Velés to believe it, Juliette will know he isn't really related.

"Your grandfather?" Mr. Velés asks. Juliette, too, furrows her brow.

"Yup." The key to a good lie is committing to it, so that's what I do. "He just arrived in town to visit me, and I believe he was headed to Chicago anyway. I'll ask him tonight to take us along."

Mr. Velés sits a moment in silence studying me, as if he can read the lie etched across my face, but I don't back down. I need to protect Juliette, and if lies are the only way to do it, that's what I'll do.

Slowly, the tired old magician nods. Juliette reaches over and squeezes his wrinkled hand. "Thank you."

"I can't be your chaperone!" Dr. Wells insists when I finally find him that night. The moon is full and round above us as we stand in the shadows of the stage, empty since the day Viggo died.

"You have to. You sent me back here to protect her, and I can't do that if she's hundreds of miles away. You know the societal norms of this time—it'd ruin her reputation to be traveling around the country alone with a young man who isn't her husband. You do this for me, and as soon as we find a new magician, I'll give you that journal."

Dr. Wells startles. "So you *do* have it!"

"Not yet. But I know where it is." Well, I have some idea. I've already checked the storage boxes where Juliette found it, and since it isn't there, she must still have it. She must have forgotten about it in the wake of Viggo's death, which means it's probably still in her wagon. It shouldn't be difficult to find—there are only so many places to put it in such a small space—so all I need are a few minutes to search for it while she isn't around.

"You don't leave me much choice, do you?" Dr. Wells asks.

"I'm only trying to do what you've told me."

Dr. Wells wrings his hands. "She must be very important then, if I've sent you back here to protect her."

"Yeah." She is important. And I can't deny that she's been growing more and more important to me every day—with every smile, every laugh, every look. With every walk on the beach and every day in her presence. This isn't just about saving Elise and my own timeline anymore. If anything were to happen to Juliette... I can't even bear to think about it.

Dr. Wells sighs. "All right. I'll accompany you two to Chicago. But we must find Mr. Velés a new magician quickly; I don't know what else is going on here—"

I open my mouth, but Dr. Wells interrupts.

"No," he says. "I don't want to know more than I already do, but the fact that there are two time travelers here from two different eras—"

I don't mention the TUB agent, here from a third.

"—well, I don't like it. The potential is high for a disaster with long-reaching consequences, ones that extend far beyond this time. No, I think the sooner we get back to our own eras, the better."

CHAPTER TWELVE

When I introduce Dr. Wells to Mr. Velés the next morning, Juliette is sitting with him at a makeshift breakfast table outside the wagons.

"This is my grandfather," I say, introducing the older men and meeting Juliette's gaze over the rim of her coffee mug. She narrows her eyes at me but doesn't say a word. I'd hoped she wouldn't let a little white lie get in the way of her own goals, and it seems I was right. It isn't until after the two older men are deep in conversation about some place they'd each been in upstate New York that Juliette sets down her mug and addresses me.

"Chandler, would you mind walking with me to fetch a fresh bucket of water?"

"Sure, sure." I smile and tip my hat to the other men, who hardly seem to notice us, they're so deep in their conversation.

"Do you really mean for me to believe that Dr. Wells is your grandfather?" she hisses when we're out of earshot. I have to hurry to keep up with her.

"No, actually, I thought that once we were on our way, he could pose as yours. Isn't a chaperone supposed to be a relative of the woman's?"

We've reached the water pump at the edge of the fairgrounds, and

Juliette scoffs as she places the bucket beneath it. "Chaperones. I appreciate Mr. Velés's concern, but it's an outdated notion. I'm a working woman, not some delicate heiress."

"Still… you don't mind if Dr. Wells comes along, do you? Pretends to be your grandfather, for the sake of appearances? Here, let me pump that for you."

She sighs and steps to the side, still holding the bucket as water gushes into it from the pump. "No, I suppose that will be fine, since it seems everyone's insistent. Besides, I'd love to hear more of his ideas of science and time travel and what the future might hold. I wonder what he'd think of that journal I found?"

The journal. I have to get it from Juliette before Dr. Wells discovers she has it. Once he gets his hands on it, I'll have no bargaining chip to ensure his continued help.

"I don't think I'd mention it to him," I say slowly. The rusty pump handle creaks to a stop.

"Why not?"

Think, Chandler, think. I scramble to come up with some excuse. "Well, it's not really yours to share, is it?"

Juliette looks away, her cheeks reddening. "You think I should return it. Put it back where I found it."

"I'm sure Mr. Velés wouldn't mind you borrowing it, but some of the information in it seems rather important. It might be better if fewer people knew about it."

"You're probably right." Juliette picks up the bucket. "It'll just be our secret then."

"You do plan on bringing it with you to Chicago, though, don't you?"

"Do you think I ought to? I'd hate for anything to happen to it. And what if Mr. Velés goes looking for it and finds it missing? I ought to at least ask him if I can borrow it."

"I think he's got plenty of other things to worry about right now. Here, let me take that bucket."

Juliette considers the offer, then passes the water to me. "I'm glad you're coming with me. It makes me feel safer. *You* make me feel safer."

A lump forms in my throat. Regardless of what happens in Chicago... No matter what it takes... I can't let her down.

The train pulls out of the Michigan Central Railroad depot early the next morning.

I can't take my eyes from Juliette, who's practically luminous, nearly bursting with excitement as the engine picks up speed. It's the happiest I've seen her since Viggo's death, and I'm relieved that that part of her hasn't been destroyed by all that's happened. She leans out the open window to wave goodbye to Mr. Velés, who's seeing us off from the platform. On the seat beside me, Dr. Wells unwraps a candy, pops it in his mouth, and settles back with his hat pulled over his eyes to doze.

"I've never been on a train before," Juliette confides when she catches me staring. "It's fascinating, really, how quickly one can travel nowadays from one part of the country to another. Have you ever been in a more wonderful contraption?"

Dr. Wells chuckles from beneath his hat's rim, and I can tell he's thinking of how much faster travel is in his time of racecars and airplanes and space shuttles. I smile, imagining what he'd say about the travel of the 22nd century, which is twice as fast as that.

"Oh, yes," he says. "It's amazing, all right."

Juliette smiles her brilliant smile and turns back to the window. She rests her arm on the sill and—with wide, dreamy eyes—watches as we flee from the cornfields, from the recent tragedy, from the time traveler who wishes to do her harm. I fight the urge to reach out and grab her hand, to reassure her that this time... this time I'll make certain she's safe.

The brand-new, nine-story Central Station glimmers before us as the train slows to a stop. Even though I've seen plenty of impressive buildings in my day, I'm drawn to the shining structure and the clock tower that rises proudly over it all. "ILLINOIS CENTRAL," the signs declare brightly through the early evening gloom, and all around us, the city bustles in gas-lit activity.

"It's gorgeous," Juliette breathes, and though I'm not sure if she's referring to the station itself or the city in general, I have to agree. I grew up here, but still, the city is new and unexpected. This skyline is small and unfamiliar, devoid of the Sears Tower (I'll always think of it as that, regardless of what other names it goes by), the John Hancock Center, or any of the other notable sights I'm used to. What would this strange, diminished city look like from the air, flying into the not-yet-established O'Hare Airport?

Of the three of us, Dr. Wells seems most at home in this strange city, and thus is the first to pick up his bags, make his way to the aisle, and say, "Well, come on, then. Let's find our lodging before it gets too late."

Fortunately, Mr. Velés knows people in Chicago and sent us with a letter of introduction to a boarding house to the north, in what, in my early life, was known as Old Town, but which is in this time referred to as "The Cabbage Patch," thanks to the fields of potatoes, celery, and cabbage planted by the German immigrants who settled there. It's a fair distance from Jackson Park, but everything in closer proximity to the fair was already booked well in advance. Night is falling as we hop two street cars to get there, breezing up Lake Shore Drive, past what will someday be Millennium Park and Navy Pier.

"This is where you grew up, isn't it?" Juliette leans in and asks.

"How long has it been since you've been back?"

Considering there's a hundred eighteen years between then and now…
"About ten years."

"Is it the same as you remember?"

How can I answer a question like that? There's nothing familiar, nothing that resembles this city in my time. All my old familiar landmarks are gone, though not in the way things are in the future— replaced by something better, brighter, shinier, newer. No, here they're simply erased, rewound. Dr. Wells watches me, as if he, too, is wondering how I'll respond.

"The lake is the same," I say, though even that isn't necessarily true. The lake of my childhood was full of ships and yachts and glimmered in the night with the reflection of city lights. This one seems so empty, its shores relatively unadorned, and I'm suddenly filled with longing for people I haven't thought about in years: Grandparents, long dead, who walked me down to Navy Pier to ride the Ferris wheel. My mother, who worked in a building that looked out over the lake and would let me sit in her office and stare out the window on summer days when I was off school and my usual babysitter was ill. Childhood friends whose names I can't even recall, running through the blue-tinged corridors of the Shedd Aquarium on school field trips, making faces at the sharks and jellyfish.

And I want to share these things. I want to tell Juliette. But I can't.

It's a life I left behind, a world I deserted without a second thought, and it's taken coming here to make me realize that I'm never going to find anyone I can really talk to about all I've been through. Anyone who'd understand.

"There," I say, nearly leaping to my feet as I spot something familiar. It sends a strange thrill through me, like I've run into an old friend, and I laugh. "The Water Tower! It's still here!"

It stands there on the street, just like it did in my own time: a limestone structure with Gothic battlements, parapets, and spires that, as a child, I'd always thought made it look like a tiny castle huddling in the shadows of the modern giants of Michigan Avenue. Now, however, it's the tallest structure on the street, making it stand out all the more.

"It's one of few buildings that survived the Great Fire," Dr. Wells explains to Juliette, who nods politely. Her gaze, though, is fixed on me, rather than the building.

"Are you all right?" Juliette whispers, as if sensing something more in my sudden outburst. She tucks her hand in the crook of my arm, and I cover it with my own.

"It's nothing," I say, forcing a smile. "Just nostalgia."

CHAPTER THIRTEEN

The boarding house is owned by a middle-aged woman known as Mrs. Rosebloom, who seems to take her surname to heart as decorating guidelines as well. The three-story building is decked out with rosebud-patterned wallpaper, furniture with rosebud embellishments, and even windows with rosebuds etched in the glass. Mrs. Rosebloom resides on the second floor, and from there she keeps a close eye—she assures us—on the comings and goings of the men residing on the first floor and the women residing on the third.

"There will be no funny business here," she warns us, glaring at me in particular. I just grin. Despite her penchant for floral décor, Mrs. Rosebloom has the scrappy, solid appearance of a boxer. No, I won't be crossing her.

When morning arrives, Mrs. Rosebloom invites us to breakfast in her bright, floral-adorned dining room, and—not wanting to get on her bad side—I immediately concede, even though I'd rather get started on our task right away. Dr. Wells has agreed to visit the newspaper offices and place the ads which Juliette wrote on the train, while the two of us plan to gather our stack of flyers and head to the Columbian Exposition itself. There, we'll scope out the men hanging around the midway, strike up conversations about the shows, and arrange auditions for those who have a knack for magic and a desire to travel. All we need is a place to hold the auditions, and—as I enter Mrs. Rosebloom's parlor—I decide it will do quite nicely.

"Mrs. Rosebloom," I say, putting on my most charming smile. "What a lovely home you have here."

"It's been in my family for generations," she says, ushering me to the breakfast table, where we find a spread of scrambled eggs, sweet rolls, and platters of fruit. "It was built by my great-grandfather, first house in the neighborhood. Used to have a clear view to the lake from the widow's walk."

I nod appreciatively as I load up my plate. After weeks of fairground food and watery stew, I'm eager to have something with a little more substance. Across the table, Juliette's already nibbling on a piece of toast with jam, and Dr. Wells stirs cream into his tea.

"Mrs. Rosebloom," I say, "I was hoping that we might make use of your parlor as we interview candidates for the position we're trying to fill. None of the rented rooms are large enough for a proper display of magic, and that way, you could watch as well... be our test audience. What do you think?"

Mrs. Rosebloom purses her lips, and for a moment, I worry she might say no.

"Yes, I suppose that will do," she says. "Though you'll need to inform me ahead of time so that I might have refreshments prepared."

"Refreshments?"

"Well, I can't possibly host a show without refreshments. I've a dozen ladies in my quilting circle; I suppose I'll have to set up the chairs on the outside edges of the room so you have plenty of room for your show."

"I... A dozen? For the show?"

"That doesn't seem fair to you? Use of my parlor in exchange for a bit of amusement for a few old biddies?"

Juliette smiles at me over her coffee mug. She looks as though she's fighting back laughter.

"Sure," I say, throwing up my arms. "Why not?"

"Good." Mrs. Rosebloom wipes the corner of her mouth with a napkin embroidered with—what else?—a rosebud. "More coffee?"

After we've eaten our fill, Juliette offers to remain behind and help Mrs. Rosebloom clean up the breakfast things.

"We won't be long," she promises, and the two women smile as though they've just been itching to get us men out of the dining room so they can discuss us privately.

Dr. Wells chatters about his plans for the day: "First stop will be the *Tribune*'s office, of course, to place those advertisements. Let's see… 1893. No *Chicago World* or *Examiner* yet, though the *Herald* is still in print, so I ought to stop there as well. I could wait with you until Miss Argent is ready to leave—"

Suddenly, I have an idea.

"No, no. You go on ahead," I say. "I believe I forgot something up in Mrs. Rosebloom's parlor."

"Indeed?" Dr. Wells raises his eyebrow. It's a feeble excuse and I know it doesn't fool him, but he sighs and waves me away. "Well, go on then with whatever it is that you need to do. I shall meet you two for dinner, correct?"

"We'll be there," I promise.

As soon as Dr. Wells descends the stairs, I turn and head the other way, careful to keep my footfalls light. As I pass Mrs. Rosebloom's door on the second floor, I press my ear to it just long enough to ensure that Juliette is still inside. I don't like the thought of snooping through her things, but when else am I going to get an opportunity to search for the journal?

Juliette's voice is muffled through the door, but I feel like I'd know it anywhere. "Whatever do you mean, Mrs. Rosebloom?"

"I see the way you two look at one another." Our hostess's words are harder to make out, and the next ones I don't catch at all, though from the tone, it sounds as though she ends with a question.

"I don't know," Juliette says. "To be honest, there's a lot I don't know about him. I wish I did. I can't help but feel that he's hiding something from me."

I step away from the door, my heart heavy. The uncertainty in her voice pains me. There are so many things I wish I could tell her, but I can't.

It's hard to pull myself away, but I don't know how much time I have, so I race up the stairs and turn the knob of Juliette's door carefully, praying she didn't bother to lock it when she went down to breakfast. Fortunately, it opens with barely a creak.

I scour her sitting room first, pulling open the table drawer and sifting through the pockets of Juliette's coat. By the time I finish, I'm sweating, and—irritated—I throw my own coat on the chair where I'll be sure to see it before leaving.

In the back room, I search beneath the canopy bed and in the dresser drawers before reluctantly turning to Juliette's trunk. Somehow opening that seems a greater invasion of her privacy than looking in Mrs. Rosebloom's furnishings, but I have to find that journal for Dr. Wells.

I kneel beside the trunk and its lock clicks open easily beneath my fingers. Neatly folded clothing takes up half the space inside—soft swatches of cotton and muslin and a silk gown I've never seen on her, all smelling of heady lavender. On the other side are books and other personal effects. I turn them over reverently, reading each of the books' titles, wondering how many times she's read each one, which is her favorite, and how I might bring them up in conversation without admitting to snooping.

Finally, I find the journal, tucked between Jules Verne's *From the Earth to the Moon* and Jane C. Loudon's *The Mummy!: Or a Tale of the Twenty-Second Century*. The irony is not lost on me.

I flip through the pages, searching for the one that's lost in Dr. Wells's time. There, in the back, whole and clear and undamaged is the image of the Wormhole Device.

There's a noise in the other room, and, panicking, I tear out the page opposite it, which is filled with equations entirely indecipherable to me and I shove it in my pocket. I toss the book into her trunk, bringing the lid down gently just as a figure steps into the doorway.

Juliette.

I draw in my breath, bracing for anger and irritation. She has every right to be offended, but when she meets my eye, her expression is one of wide-eyed wonder.

"I'm so sorry—" I begin, but then I see that she's holding my jacket in one hand and the shining black orb of the Wormhole Device in the other. Her gaze flickers from the device to her trunk, where the journal with its matching illustration lies.

"Take me with you," she says.

CHAPTER FOURTEEN

"Take you...?"

"I know what this is," she holds out the device. "I know what its purpose is, and now it makes so much sense. Where you've come from, all the strange things you've said, that entire discussion with Dr. Wells at the tavern. You're from the *future*."

My mouth feels dry. This is not how this is supposed to go. But I can't lie. Not to her. "I can't."

"Can't what? Can't tell me?" She settles her hands on her hips. "Or can't take me with you?"

"Look." I run my fingers through my hair. I'm completely unprepared for this conversation. "I can't explain everything. In fact, I don't think I can really explain *anything* else without breaking the rules—"

"There's rules? What are they? Do people frequently time travel where you're from? *When* you're from," she corrects herself.

"No. No, this... it's a well-kept secret. Hardly anyone knows it's possible and the few who do aren't allowed to discuss it. I shouldn't be talking about this. Not here. Not now."

"How far into the future are you from?" Juliette asks. "At least tell me that much."

It's a simple question, or at least it should be. "Technically? About a hundred years."

Juliette raises her eyebrows and whispers, "A hundred years. We must seem so primitive to you."

"No, not at all. In fact—"

"Viggo," Juliette says sharply. "Did you know that was going to happen? That he was going to—"

"Absolutely not."

"Then why are you here? Why here? Why now? What makes this time, this place so important?"

"I can't say any more right now, but once all this is over…"

Juliette frowns. "So, you can't say any more, and you won't take me with you. How long do you intend to stay?"

"I don't know."

Juliette looks away, her frustration and disappointment apparent.

"I'll stay as long as I can," I promise. "And before I leave, I'll tell you as much as I can. I swear. I wish I could say more, but…"

But what good would it do her to know what I know about her future? What good would it do to tell her that her life is in danger because of something her great-great-granddaughter did? Because she saved my life?

"You're going to leave, then?"

"Not yet." At the hurt in her eyes, I begin to wish I'd never have to. What would it be like, remaining here with her? But, no. Dodge is waiting for me back home in the 22nd century.

"Just promise me," she says, unable to meet my eye as she holds out the Wormhole Device, "that when it's time for you to go, you won't forget to say goodbye."

My hand touches hers as I take the orb. "I swear, Juliette, I won't."

The famous White City of the 1893 World's Fair rises up before us as Juliette and I ride the crowded El Train to the Exposition. Since our discussion in her room, Juliette is quieter than usual, but every so often, as if she can't even help herself, she leans in and whispers excitedly about some of the things she hopes to see there—the Women's Building, the replica Viking ship, the moving sidewalk—and then, as if recalling our purpose, quickly adds, "After we've found a magician, of course."

Eventually, I can't help but suggest, "You know, we could spend the morning looking about and then hand out our flyers in the afternoon."

"Could we, you think?" Juliette smiles as if I've just offered her the moon.

"Why not? It's a once-in-a-lifetime opportunity."

"I'd like that. We ought to see Ferris's Wheel, too."

I cringe, thinking of how primitive the constructions of this time are, how creaking and shaky the thing must be.

"It's perfectly safe, you know," she says with a hint of teasing in her voice. "They have precautions in place—locks on the doors, metal screens over the windows. You'll like it. I promise."

We join the throng funneling into the fair from the train platform, and the enormous Transportation Building looms over us with arch after perfect arch standing out against the otherwise classical-style architecture.

"What do you think? Should we go see the Railways of the World exhibit?" I ask, offering Juliette my arm. The smile she gives me is warier than usual, a small difference that tears at my heart and makes me wish again that I could tell her everything.

The morning sun traverses the sky all too quickly, and when noon comes, we've barely seen a fraction of all that the fair has to offer. We skipped the Mines Building but lingered for far too long in the Electricity Building—built in the style of the Spanish Renaissance—as Juliette marveled over neon lights and Tesla's alternating currents and the 82-foot "tower of light" made of shimmering bits of cut glass. From there, we ducked onto the wooded island and wandered the paths around the lagoon, enjoying the cool shade of the trees in the heat of the day and the less-crowded Hunter's Cabin and Japanese Pavilions. There, we sit on a bench, watching the crowds pass as we rest our weary feet.

"What about that man with the top hat?" Juliette asks, pointing to a gentleman who'd just passed us on the walk.

"What about him?"

"He looks like he'd make a fine magician."

I shake my head. "He looks too uptight to me."

"What do you suppose his life story is? His goals, ambitions? Why is he here today?"

"I don't know. He looks like a businessman to me." I lean back and cross one leg over the other, breathing in the scent of summer flowers and the lagoon. A breeze ripples over my skin, and everything feels so peaceful, so *right* that for a moment, I forget the tension of our discussion this morning. I forget that I don't belong here, with her.

Juliette frowns, obviously disappointed by my answer. "Well, what's he doing here, then, if he really is just a businessman? On a weekday when he ought to be at work?"

"He's probably here on his lunch break." Then, in an attempt to make her smile—a desire that's been growing stronger every day, regardless of how much I try to tell myself, logically, that it's a dangerous pursuit—I add. "Either that, or he's an undercover detective who's made arrangements to meet an anonymous informant today regarding information about a murder case."

"Yes!" Juliette beams at me. "That's perfect. It's obviously a long unsolved case, one very personal to him: the murder of his former lover. Though the informant doesn't know that, of course."

"Of course."

"What about those women?" Juliette gestures slyly to a group of women—perhaps in their late thirties or early forties—all walking together with arms linked, clinging to their bonnets and laughing and chattering merrily.

They look like any ordinary group of women out enjoying a day at the fair, but with Juliette's eyes twinkling at me like that, I can't let her down. "Suffragists."

"Suffragists?" Juliette nudges me playfully with her elbow. "Well, that's hardly worth noting. Plenty of women are suffragists, myself included."

"Oh, these aren't just any suffragists," I continue. "These are an elite group of suffragist spies—black widows, who've sworn a pact to marry themselves off to the most influential and wealthy gentlemen in society and then poison them to gain complete access to their resources."

"Scandalous!" Juliette shrieks with laughter, and I'm overcome with relief that finally, it seems, she's forgotten—if not forgiven—my secrets. "What about him, then? That fellow on that bench there. The one with the prominent nose. He's been sitting there all alone since shortly after we arrived, just reading that pamphlet. He must have some story."

I lean forward to glance around her, pausing briefly to admire the masterful shape of her profile before focusing on the man at the bench.

Even from this distance, I can make out his face, wearing a mustache that looks itchy, not quite right for him, as though he's unaccustomed to wearing one. His long legs are stretched out ahead of him, and it takes me a moment to realize where I've seen him before, a moment to recognize the band on his wrist.

"TUB."

CHAPTER FIFTEEN

"TUB?" Juliette asks. "What's TUB?"

I pull her to her feet. Out of the corner of my eye, the TUB agent tucks his pamphlet into his jacket.

"You're going to have to trust me on this one," I say. "We have to lose him."

How did he find us anyway? Has he been trailing us since Saginaw, just waiting in the shadows for an opportunity? I think back to our actions over the past days—the train tickets we bought, the guest book we signed at Mrs. Rosebloom's, the flyers we've been half-heartedly handing out throughout the day—all ways that someone in the future could track us to this time and place.

"Is this part of the game?" Juliette asks, her expression a mix of confusion and amusement.

I still can't figure out how to answer her. It'd be easy to tell her that it's a game, make her believe the danger is only an illusion, but would that be fair? I hate the thought of lying to her.

Together we dash down the wooded pathway toward the bridge leading off the island. We have to get back to the rest of the fair, where we can melt into the bustling crowds and disappear.

"Chandler? What's going on?" Juliette asks, struggling to keep up.

"Does this have to do with… with where you're from?"

"Afraid so."

"Why? Who is he? What does he want with us?"

"I'll explain later." I stop and look around. The Women's Building looms before us, and beyond that, Ferris's wheel rises up like an enormous bicycle tire on the midway. The midway. We can lose the man among the crowd. "This way."

One thing's for certain, the midway is busy—a chaotic jumble of entertainers and spectators, of colorful flags and exotic costumes, of scents and sights and music and dancing. Even if we weren't evading a homicidal time traveler, it'd still be a struggle to stay together in the dense crowd.

We rush down the street, passing the nursery exhibits, the log cabin, the Irish village, the Dutch settlement, until finally I pull Juliette into the shadows of a German castle. All around its courtyard, people meander about, taking in the sights. An orchestra plays in the grandstand. Couples are bowling in horseshoe-shaped alleys, and the scent of beer is sharp and heavy in the air.

Inside the stone arches of the castle, it's darker and quieter, but I still don't feel safe. Music echoes around us, and Juliette leans in close—so close that I'm momentarily overwhelmed by the scent of lavender. She whispers in my ear.

"Tell me. Please. Why is that man after you?"

I hesitate. I'm not going to lie, but I have to say something. "I don't know him personally, but he's part of a dangerous organization—"

"From your time?"

"Yes, one that I've had some trouble with before." No need to mention that I worked for the scumbags. "They're not people to take lightly. You must promise me that if you see him again, you'll get out. Wherever you are, whatever you're doing, just run."

"What do they want with you?"

When had I taken her hands? I'm lost for a moment in their

warmth, their texture, the smoothness of each curved nail. It's strange that I can have such a strong desire—such a *need*—to protect this woman whom I've only known a few weeks, who was born a century before my time, but I do.

"What do they want?" Juliette repeats, pulling me from my mind's wild ramblings.

"I promise someday I'll tell you—"

Juliette raises her eyebrows, and I bite my tongue. What am I doing, making promises to her? I don't even know how long I'll be able to stay here. I never asked Dr. Wells how I'd know when Juliette is truly safe. Even if I get rid of this guy, how can I ensure TUB won't send another agent after her? And another? And another?

"We need to get back to Mrs. Rosebloom's," I say. I have to talk to Dr. Wells, to tell this version of the man *everything*, including where to find the journal page with the instructions he needs, which I'd tucked away in my suitcase beneath my bed in the boarding house. I can't do this on my own, not anymore. I'd thought that bringing Juliette to Chicago would be safer, but if TUB's followed us here, I've obviously underestimated them. Again.

"But what about these?" Juliette holds up the flyers. "If we don't hand them out today, we'll just have to come back tomorrow."

"Right. Here's what we'll do." I gather a handful of the ads. "We'll find someone else to distribute them for us. There's got to be some young boys running around here, eager to make a few dollars."

"A few dollars?" Juliette's eyes widen. "How much do you intend to pay them?"

How much *is* a dollar worth in 1893? I must have grossly misestimated to illicit that sort of response, but I don't have time to deal with mathematical conversions, at least not right now.

"Or a quarter or two," I say hurriedly. "Do you think that would be enough?"

"Plenty. Look, what about them?" She gestures toward the bowling alley, where a trio of boys about Dodge's age are playing around with the pins and heckling one another.

Dodge. Another reason to end this thing sooner rather than later.

"Stay here," I say. Leaving Juliette in the shadows, I pull my hat low over my eyes and casually approach the boys. Fortunately, these 19th century kids aren't all too different from Dodge and his friends in the 22st century, and it doesn't take much to convince them to set aside their horseplay for an hour or so to find the nearest magic show—"or the Brothers Houdini, if you can find it"—and hand out flyers to the audience. In exchange, I offer them each two shiny quarters, which ought to be more than enough compensation.

They rush out of the German village, clutching their money in one hand and the flyers in the other. Hopefully they won't just chuck the flyers into the nearest waste bin as soon as they're out of sight. Even so, we'd still have Dr. Wells's newspaper advertisements. In fact, maybe we could send Dr. Wells back to the fair in the following days, and Juliette and I can pick up where he left off with the newspapers. Somehow, that seems safer.

I turn back to the castle, expecting to see her slim figure in the shadows of the entrance, but the archway is empty. My gut flips and I glance around. Did she see the TUB agent and slip inside, deeper into the castle's protection? The man's nowhere to be seen, but then again, neither is Juliette.

"Juliette?" I call out. Fairgoers bustle around me, but none with her familiar bright smile, none with her shining eyes. My vision adjusts to the darkness of the castle, but her face doesn't greet me. She's gone.

CHAPTER SIXTEEN

They must have snuck up behind her. They must have gagged her somehow, or I would've heard her scream. The thought of the TUB agent's hands on her makes me boil with a hot fury. But where did they take her? It can't be far, or surely someone would have noticed Juliette struggling.

I rush onto the street and look around at the Javanese Settlement to the east... the Turkish Village directly across the way... and then I turn to the west, where Ferris's giant wheel looms over me.

I take off running to the Ferris wheel before I even have a chance to sort through why. Somehow it seems like an obvious place: somewhere crowded, confined, where Juliette wouldn't be able to escape.

At the platform, six cars are being loaded at once, and a uniformed guard is opening the door of the nearest one to allow passengers aboard. Each is the size of a railroad boxcar and looks like a suspended screened-in-porch. I crane my neck to see above the crowd. At the head of the line, among the first to climb into the car, is the TUB agent. And tucked against his side, with one arm gripped in his, is Juliette. Something metal flashes from inside his coat. A gun? A knife? I try to shout, but my voice is lost in the crowd.

Each car holds about sixty people, and I frantically try to estimate the size of the line, try to push ahead so that I'm on the same car. I don't know what the agent has in mind, but to have any chance at all of stopping it, I have to be in that car.

"Excuse me. Pardon me. I need to catch up with my party." I shove past the other fairgoers, who shoot me irritated looks. Never mind them. I don't have time for pleasantries. From out of nowhere, a guard steps forward.

"No more room," he says, moving to close the door. "You'll have to take the next car."

"No, no, no." I peer out over the crowd. I want to tell the guard about the weapon, but Juliette and the agent are on the other end of the car; if I say anything now, it'll cause a panic. There's no way I'll get to them before he harms her. Thinking fast, I force a smile. "You don't understand. I have to be on this car."

"Is that so? And why's that?"

"Ahh… my girl, you see. She's on this car."

The guard raises an eyebrow. "Why isn't she with you, if she's your girl?"

"Well, she's not mine yet," I admit. "But I've never met a girl like her, and she's in this car, and you wouldn't deny me a chance to tell her how important she is to me, would you?"

I'm laying it on thick, but something about my desperate plea must resonate with the guard, because he sighs and slides the door open just far enough for me to squeeze in. "Go on in. You've got two times around."

"Thank you so much, sir." I shove a handful of coins at him and step into the car.

The car lurches to a start, creaking and groaning every bit as loudly as I'd expected. The passengers press their faces against the windows, gazing out in awe as we ascend. It takes a moment for my eyes to adjust to the lower light, and even then, I don't see Juliette.

I work my way across the car, saying, "Excuse me," and "Pardon me," to each person I squeeze past. I'm halfway across the car's twenty-six feet before I spot the back of Juliette's head. The TUB agent is still standing beside her, holding her firmly to his side. From this close, I can see the outline of his pistol clearly, its barrel pressed into Juliette's ribs. The two of them are standing against the far door, and the TUB agent is muttering something to Juliette. I don't know what he's waiting for—why he hasn't shot her already. I just have to get to her before he does.

The passengers press in on me on all sides, and I feel oppressed by the closeness of the car, the presence of all these strangers who have nothing on their mind but enjoying the view of the Midway Palisades. They didn't ask to be locked in here, 250 feet above the city, with a madman, a time traveler, and a woman on whose fate his future is hinged. But how can I rescue Juliette without putting more people in harm's way?

As we crest the top of the wheel, a rattling noise makes my stomach drop. Anyone else in the car might think it's merely one of the many rumblings of the giant wheel's spokes, but I can see the TUB agent tugging at the handle of the door.

In the next second, the man has Juliette pressed against it, with the lock disengaged and only his hand holding it closed behind her. She glares at him and spits in his face, and, like her, I throw caution to the wind. I rush forward.

She sees me and her eyes light with a glimmer of hope, just as the TUB agent releases the door and elbows her out.

I push other passengers aside. Beside me, someone screams at the sight of the door flying open. No one else sees the TUB agent reach into his pocket and press the button on a shining black device. No one else sees as he disappears. All eyes are on Juliette as she tumbles backward, arms pinwheeling like the spokes of the Ferris wheel, and then falling, screaming, toward the ground below.

Somehow, I grab her hand, and for a moment, I think I might be able to save her. Our fingers entwine, but instead of slowing her momentum, it only yanks me forward, out the open doorway. My fingers grip the doorframe for a second... two seconds... just long enough for me to look below, to where Juliette clings to me and her desperate eyes plead.

"Don't let go." Her voice sounds small, yet firm, as though she might, by the mere force of her will, keep us from falling.

I won't.

The wheel lurches, and as my fingers slip from the metal frame, I don't care anymore about the past or future. I don't care about the repercussions. I know what I have to do.

The brilliant blue Chicago sky falls past. Lake Michigan hovers somewhere beyond, and in the half an instant it takes for me to marvel that it's still the same shoreline I'd last seen from a 747, I reach inside my jacket.

I pull Juliette close, clinging to her like a lifeline, and press the small, thumb-sized button on my Wormhole Device.

The world bursts into light.

CHAPTER SEVENTEEN: JUNE 22, 2016

We land in a jumble of arms, legs, and skirts on Dr. Wells's sofa. I leap to my feet, tripping over Juliette's skirt and tumbling onto the floor, knocking over a pile of dossiers and sending papers scattering to the floor.

Juliette jerks upright. "Am I dead?"

"No." I hold up the Wormhole Device. "You're in the year 2016."

"2016?" With a deep, steadying breath, Juliette looks around the office, her eyes falling on each unfamiliar item: the telephone on Dr. Wells's desk, which I'd always thought looked like it belonged in a museum; the desktop computer with its swirling screen saver dancing across the screen; even little things like the mechanical pencils and the coffeemaker on the side table. I see them now through Juliette's eyes, and realize, for the first time, how fascinating these mundane things truly are, how all these things I'd taken for granted are really miracles of technology, part of a bright, glimmering future.

If she's amazed by this, what would she think of the 22nd century? Now that we're here, now that I've thrown caution to the wind and broken all the rules anyway, I want, more than anything, to find out. But first, I need to find out how much Dr. Wells already knew when he sent me on this mission.

"Are you all right?" I help Juliette to her feet.

"I'm incredible!" She laughs. "I'm in the future! This is amazing. Are we still in Chicago?"

"No, my dear, you're in New York City." The voice that answers from the doorway is Dr. Wells's, sounding tired and somewhat resigned as he enters the room.

"And you must be—" Juliette turns to face him and stops short. "Dr. Wells? But how?" She looks back and forth between the two of us and bursts out laughing again. "You're a time traveler, too! I should have known!"

"Dr. Wells was looking for that journal you found," I explain before he can stop me. "He's the one who created the time travel device that I used to go back to 1893. The one who sent me there in the first place, to protect you from TUB."

"To protect *me*?" Juliette asks. "But why would they be after me? I thought they were looking for you."

"I didn't want to tell you, though I see now I should have. It might have made a difference back at the fair."

"The only reason I went so quietly was because I thought I was helping lead that monster away from you," she says. "But why me?"

"One of your descendants," I begin, "gets tangled up in their web a hundred years from now, and when they can't trace her, they go after you instead, trying to destroy her family line so she'll never be born."

"But when I met you...?" Juliette starts, looking to Dr. Wells.

"I didn't know then," Dr. Wells says. "I was only just beginning to delve into the depths of time travel when I first met you. 1893 was the first place in the past I'd ever traveled, and it was certainly an experience I will never forget."

"You found the journal page in my suitcase?" I ask.

"Oh, yes," Dr. Wells says, sounding none too pleased. "I suppose now I might finally get an opportunity to find out what exactly happened to you that day when you disappeared."

"Disappeared?" Juliette looks to me, as though I might have some explanation, but I don't.

"Yes. You left Mrs. Rosebloom's boarding house that morning and never returned. We searched for weeks but never found a trace of you."

"But the Ferris Wheel," I say. "We fell hundreds of feet. Surely someone saw that."

"Yes, a bunch of boys whom you'd sent to hand out flyers. They believed it was all part of a magic trick and told everyone as much."

"Oh!" Juliette's hand flies to her face. "What about Mr. Velés?"

"Yes, well." Dr. Wells wipes his glasses on the hem of his shirt. "Fortunately, your little stunt stirred up plenty of interest. Mrs. Rosebloom and I held the auditions ourselves, and the Amazing Velés continued his show for the next two decades, or so I've heard."

"Thank goodness," Juliette says. "I never… that is, it wasn't our intention to leave."

"Oh?" Dr. Wells looks pointedly at our entwined hands. "Mrs. Rosebloom was convinced that the two of you eloped."

Juliette blushes, but neither of us let go of one another, even as I explain how the TUB agent tracked us to the fair and tried to make it look like she accidentally tumbled from the wheel.

"You see," Juliette says, "Chandler saved my life, by bringing me here."

"And what's more," I say, "TUB doesn't know there was another time traveler there, so they'll have no reason to search for her in other timelines."

"Do you mean…?" Juliette asks. "I could stay here?"

"Oh, no." Dr. Wells shakes his head and paces behind his desk. "No, no. This won't do. Not at all. Not here. That'll never do."

"No, it certainly won't." I turn to Juliette and take her other hand. "Juliette, I love you, and I want to spend my life with you. Please, come with me. Come with me into the future, and I'll take care of you and make sure it's all you've ever dreamed of."

Tears sparkle in Juliette's eyes, and she nods, her brilliant smile beaming up at me. "The future?"

"Yes. Well, that's another thing. I don't actually live here anymore. I live a hundred years further into the future, but in a way, that's better, right? TUB would never think to look for you there. And we have gyms there where you can take acrobatics classes seven days a week if you like. And there's so many more books to read than what's available in your time."

"Please, Dr. Wells," Juliette says, smiling at the old man, all the while clutching my hand. "It's the perfect solution. We were meant to be together, to do this together. I just know it."

"You know my Rules…"

"And you said at the beginning of this that we may have to break some of them," I say. "So please, just send us back to 2113. I'll take care of Juliette from there. I promise."

The old man sighs. "Come on, then. Let's get you two lovebirds over to the DeLorean Box before any of my employees starts poking around, trying to see what's going on. If they knew what I'm allowing, how many Rules I'm breaking… I'd never hear the end of it."

"How much did you know?" I ask Dr. Wells as we wait for Juliette to emerge from the back room. He happened to have another suit of synthetic fibers which, though not precisely like the one I brought with me from 2113, will do until we can purchase Juliette some appropriate clothing of her own.

"I think you know the answer to that," he says, frowning at the dials on the DeLorean Box.

"You remembered that I was there," I guess, "that you'd met me when you traveled to 1893 all those years ago. And you would have remembered how I'd felt about her and that we disappeared together.

You knew we'd end up together one way or another."

Dr. Wells nods. "Yes, well, I tried to let things play out with as little interference as possible, but you had told me, all those years ago, that I had been the one to send you there, so when I began to suspect that TUB was targeting her, I knew it was time to do what had to be done."

"How do I look?" Juliette asks as she appears in the doorway.

I can't help but smile at how strange the outfit looks on her. I'm so used to seeing her in long skirts and frilled blouses; even the risqué magician's assistant costume that she wore for the Amazing Velés's shows seemed more suitable for her than the shimmering white jumpsuit that's at least four sizes too big.

"Amazing."

A thrill goes through me as I hold open the door of the DeLorean box for her. What will she think of the world I live in? What will Dodge think of her? Maybe it's naïve of me, but it doesn't matter. I'm filled with an inexplicable sense of confidence that somehow, this is *right*, that it was meant to be all along.

Dr. Wells clears his throat, and a furrow of worry creases his brow. "I left a message in your left pocket."

"That caused quite some trouble last time," I say, chuckling. Dr. Wells's warning about TUB was what set this whole thing rolling in the first place, what convinced me to go AWOL. Had he only done that because he'd known someday he'd have to send me to the past? That my time couldn't possibly be up yet?

"Yes, well… this might cause just as much trouble, but I have confidence that it all will work out. Somehow." Despite his words, Dr. Wells doesn't look so sure. "There's a date on the envelope. Don't open it until then."

Until the point of no return, I can't help but think. It doesn't matter. Something niggles at the back of my head, something I've forgotten, some loose thread, but whatever it is, it won't—can't—change my mind about wanting Juliette with me in the future, wanting her in my life.

I step into the DeLorean box and take Juliette's hand. With the other, I wave goodbye to Dr. Wells. Only then does it hit me that this could be the last time I see the old man, and that I've grown to like him. To think of him as a friend.

Before I can say a thing, though, Dr. Wells hits the button, and as the present-day swirls out of existence around us, Juliette's smile, shining like a radiant beam, guides me home.

EPILOGUE: APRIL 15, 2113

I make every effort to ensure that Juliette's transition to the 22nd century is an easy one, but I quickly find my worries are unfounded. Within a week, she's ordering Punch-In, making transactions using retina scans, and trying to catch up on the past two hundred years' worth of history on the holographic video screens. She signs up for acrobatics classes and comes home from them each day on her hover vehicle, looking flushed with excitement and eager to share everything she's learned.

Dodge doesn't mind having Juliette around. In fact, he's more irritated with the fact that I went and spent so much time in the past without him.

"You'll take me back in time someday, won't you?" he pleads. "I never get to do anything fun."

I laugh and ruffle his hair. I can't believe how much I missed this kid.

"It's not up to me," I say. "Dr. Wells is the one with the time machines. You'll have to ask him someday."

"If we ever see him again," Juliette says.

I nod and shove a hand into my pocket, thinking of the envelope I brought back with me, which now lies at the bottom of an electronic drawer beneath my bed. I've been tempted to open it a few times, but I'm pretty sure I've worked out already what it will say, and selfishly, I'd rather not think about the logical repercussions of our decision until we have to.

Over the next months, it weighs heavily on me, even as Juliette grows more and more comfortable in her surroundings. Even as we plan our wedding, with Dodge as the best man and Juliette's acrobatics instructor—who's quickly become one of her best friends—as the maid of honor.

Still, I keep it sealed until we've been married for about six months, when Juliette sits beside me on the bed we now share and clutches my hands and tells me the good news.

I'm going to be a father.

"When is the baby due?" I ask, my throat dry. I can do the math. Has Juliette realized it, too? Realized what we've done by bringing her here? What will need to be done someday in our future?

"April. Around the fifteenth." Juliette beams. "Tianna assures me that after she gave birth, she was back on the trapeze within a few months, thanks to advancements in postpartum care. Chandler? What's wrong? Aren't you happy?"

"Of course I am. Have you told Dodge?"

"Do you think I should yet?"

"Absolutely. He'll be thrilled."

Juliette leans in and plants a kiss on my lips. The sensation still sends thrills through me. How did I get so lucky? Then she leaps from the bed, calling for Dodge. As soon as she's gone, I reach down and press the button on the under-the-bed drawer. It slides out, and there's the letter from Dr. Wells. Dated for April 15, 2115. I can't put it off any longer.

With shaking hands, I tear it open.

Dear Chandler,

If you've followed my instructions and kept this sealed until the date on the envelope, then today I must congratulate you on the birth of your daughter. I must believe that by now, you've worked out the problem with Juliette joining you in the future; you understand, perhaps, why it would not have been my choice for you two to fall in love, and yet... and yet I couldn't go against the experiences of my own past.

As you know, I've researched my Retrievers' ancestry extensively. It's necessary, in a job like mine. That's how I know that Juliette is Elise's great-great-grandmother. What I didn't know, however, was what happened to her over the next decades. You see, there are gaps in the records, as often happens in genealogical research. Juliette disappeared from history in the summer of 1893. The next appearance of Elise's family line is on a 1915 state census where a 19-year-old woman lists Juliette as her mother and her father simply as "C."

You see, your daughter must return to the 1900s, or Juliette's family line will disappear from this era. Without her presence here, there will be no Elise. And without Elise, who goes back into the past to become my very own grandmother, there will be no me.

I tell you this now, when your daughter is small, so you can decide how you wish to raise her. Whether or not you tell her that this is her destiny is up to you as her parents, but just know that eighteen years from now, I will be back, and then, she will have to return to her rightful era.

Yours through all time,
Dr. Wells

ABOUT THE AUTHOR

Wendy Nikel is a speculative fiction author with a degree in elementary education, a fondness for road trips, and a terrible habit of forgetting where she's left her cup of tea. Her short fiction has been published by *Fantastic Stories of the Imagination, Daily Science Fiction, Nature: Futures,* and elsewhere. For more info, visit wendynikel.com

ACKNOWLEDGEMENTS

Each book that is published is really a culmination of two stories: the one within the written words printed on the page, and the behind-the-scenes real-life journey the author took to get those words there. I'm incredibly grateful for all those who played a part in that latter story; you helped make this book possible.

Special thanks to my family: to my husband and boys for their patience and support; to my parents and siblings for their love and encouragement; to my church family, friends, and relatives whose eagerness and excitement for these books overwhelmed me.

Thanks to my critique partners S. L. Saboviec, Diane McIntire Rose, Nicole Mogavero, and Rebecca M. Latimer for all the critiques and encouragement, but also for sharing my excitement when writing is going well and commiserating when it's not. Thanks also to liz, CCC, and MC, as well as all the members of the Codex Writer's Group for being a great support system and resource.

Thanks to those at World Weaver Press for taking a chance on me (again!) and working hard to make this series a success: editor Rhonda Parrish, publisher Sarena Ulibarri, and publicist Kristen Bates.

And finally, a special thank you to everyone who purchased, read, and reviewed THE CONTINUUM, who requested this book at their local library and shared this story with their friends and family. To all of you who asked for a sequel, who wanted to learn more about what happens to the Place in Time travel agency, thank you for taking this journey with me!

Thank you for reading!

We hope you'll leave an honest review at Amazon, Goodreads, or wherever you discuss books online.

Leaving a review means a lot for the author and editors who worked so hard to create this book.

Please sign up for our newsletter for news about upcoming titles, submission opportunities, special discounts, & more.

WorldWeaverPress.com/newsletter-signup

CAMPAIGN 2100: GAME OF SCORPIONS
Larry Hodges

The year is 2100, and the world has adopted the American two-party electoral system. When it comes to the election for president of Earth, the father-daughter team of Toby and Lara Platt are the cutthroat campaign directors who get candidates elected by any means necessary—including the current president, Corbin Dubois of France. But when an alien lands outside the United Nations, claiming to be an ambassador from Tau Ceti, Dubois orders her attacked. Toby resigns.

The alien survives—and so, it seems, might Dubois's corrupt reelection campaign, now run by Lara. But Toby vows to put his daughter out of a job. He challenges the two major parties—one conservative, one liberal—and runs for president himself with a third-party moderate challenge. He's a long-shot, but he's determined to fix the problems he created in getting Dubois elected.

Amid rising tensions and chants of "Alien go home!" the campaign crisscrosses every continent as father and daughter battle for electoral votes and clash over the ideas and issues facing the world of 2100 in this bare-knuckle, fight-to-the-finish political campaign. The world is watching. And so is the alien.

"Larry Hodges is an insightful political commentator and a kick-ass science-fiction writer. A dynamite novel full of twists and turns; this futuristic *House of Cards* is both entertaining and thought-provoking."
—Robert J. Sawyer, Hugo and Nebula Award-winning author of *Quantum Night*

FAR ORBIT
SPECULATIVE SPACE ADVENTURES
Edited by Bascomb James

Featuring stories by award winners **Gregory Benford, Tracy Canfield, Eric Choi, David Wesley Hill**, and more, with an open letter to speculative fiction by **Elizabeth Bear**.

"Put aside all of your preconceived notions of what 'sci-fi' is—whether you think you love it or hate, it doesn't matter—pick up this book and get to reading!"

— Good Choice Reading

FAR ORBIT APOGEE
More modern space adventures
Edited by Bascomb James

Far Orbit Apogee takes all of the fun-to-read adventure, ingenuity, and heroism of mid-century pulp fiction and reshapes it into modern space adventures crafted by a new generation of writers. Follow the adventures of heroic scientists, lunar detectives, space dragons, robots, interstellar pirates, gun slingers, and other memorable and diverse characters as they wrestle with adversity beyond the borders of our small blue marble.

Featuring stories from Jennnifer Campbell-Hicks, Dave Creek, Eric Del Carlo, Dominic Dulley, Nestor Delfino, Milo James Fowler, Julie Frost, Sam S. Kepfield, Keven R. Pittsinger, Wendy Sparrow, Anna Salonen, James Van Pelt, and Jay Werkheiser.

Murder in the Generative Kitchen
Meg Pontecorvo

With the Vacation Jury Duty system, jurors can lounge on a comfortable beach while watching the trial via virtual reality. Julio is loving the beach, as well as the views of a curvy fellow juror with a rainbow-lacquered skin modification who seems to be the exact opposite of his recent ex-girlfriend back in Chicago. Because of jury sequestration rules, they can't talk to each other at all, or else they'll have to pay full price for this Acapulco vacation. Still, Julio is desperate to catch her attention. But while he struts and tries to catch her eye, he also becomes fascinated by the trial at hand.

At first it seemed a foregone conclusion that the woman on trial used a high-tech generative kitchen to feed her husband a poisonous meal, but the more evidence mounts, the more Julio starts to suspect the kitchen may have made the decision on its own.

"Mysteriously delicious. Tastefully romantic. With a GMO garnish."
—Terry Bisson, author of *Bears Discover Fire and Other Stories*

"*Murder in the Generative Kitchen* by Meg Pontecorvo is a compact little story with a lot to say. Readers will find a fresh take on Asimov's three laws, see a twisted future where vacations are paid for by the courts, and learn that the same old arguments will still be contested long after we're gone."
—Ricky L. Brown, *Amazing Stories*

"With Murder in the Generative Kitchen, new author Meg Pontecorvo cooks up and dishes out for you not one, not two, but three original sci fi premises. Enjoy and digest them well!"
—David Brin, author of *Existence* and *The Postman*

GLASS AND GARDENS: SOLARPUNK SUMMERS
Anthology
Edited by Sarena Ulibarri

Solarpunk is a type of optimistic science fiction that imagines a future founded on renewable energies. The seventeen stories in this volume are not dull utopias—they grapple with real issues such as the future and ethics of our food sources, the connection between technology and nature, and the interpersonal conflicts that arise no matter how peaceful the world is. In these pages you'll find a guerilla art installation in Milan, a murder mystery set in a weather manipulation facility, and a world where you are judged by the glow of your solar nanite implants. From an opal mine in Australia to the seed vault at Svalbard, from a wheat farm in Kansas to a crocodile ranch in Malaysia, these are stories of adaptation, ingenuity, and optimism for the future of our world and others. For readers who are tired of dystopias and apocalypses, these visions of a brighter future will be a breath of fresh air.

Featuring stories by Jaymee Goh, D.K. Mok, Julia K. Patt, Holly Schofield, Wendy Nikel, and more.

SPECULATIVE STORY BITES
Edited by Sarena Ulibarri

Fifteen bite-sized stories, offering a sampler platter of fantasy, science fiction, and paranormal horror. Within these pages, you'll find flower fairies, alien brothels, were-bears, and sentient houses. Step inside a museum where all the displays are haunted, follow a siren into the underworld as she searches for Persephone, and discover the doors that lie, literally, behind the heart.

Featuring stories by Shannon Phillips, Adam Gaylord, Rebecca Roland, Dianne Williams, M.T. Reiten, Larry Hodges, Anya J. Davis, Jamie Lackey, Megan Neumann, Kristina Wojtaszek, Gregory Scheckler, Sandi Leibowitz, Nora Mulligan, Tom Howard, and A.E. Decker.

World Weaver Press, LLC
Publishing fantasy, paranormal, and science fiction.
We believe in great storytelling.
WorldWeaverPress.com

Made in the USA
San Bernardino, CA
18 August 2018